BERKSHIRE & MIDDLESEX

Edited By Brixie Payne

First published in Great Britain in 2019 by:

 Young**Writers**

Young Writers
Remus House
Coltsfoot Drive
Peterborough
PE2 9BF
Telephone: 01733 890066
Website: www.youngwriters.co.uk

FOREWORD

Welcome, Reader!

Are you ready to step back in time? Then come right this way - your time-travelling machine awaits! It's very simple, all you have to do is turn the page and you'll be transported to the past! WOW!

Is it magic? Is it a trick? No! It's all down to the skill and imagination of primary school pupils from around the country. We gave them the task of writing a story about any time in history, and to do it in just 100 words! I think you'll agree they've achieved that brilliantly – this book is jam-packed with exciting and thrilling tales from the past.

These young authors have brought history to life with their stories. This is the power of creativity and it gives us life too! Here at Young Writers we want to pass our love of the written word onto the next generation and what better way to do that than to celebrate their writing by publishing it in a book!

It sets their work free from homework books and notepads and puts it where it deserves to be – out in the world and preserved forever! Each awesome author in this book should be super proud of themselves, and now they've got proof of their imagination, their ideas and their creativity in black and white, to look back on in years to come when their first experience of publication is an ancient adventure itself!

Now I'm off to dive through the timelines and pick some winners – it's going to be difficult to choose, but I'm going to have a lot of fun along the way. I may even learn some new history facts too!

Brixie

CONTENTS

Tej Pandey (10) 45
Khushali Pattni (10) 46
Khushi Patel (10) 47
Ravin Abhayarickrama (10) 48

Priory School, Slough

Liam Murphy (10) 49
Maya Ahmed (8) 50
Peter Veer Jennings (9) 51
Inayah Ashfaq (8) 52
Grace Gealy (9) 53
Noemi Ingrid Mistur (11) 54
Fahtima Javed (10) 55
Ghaith Al-Janabi (10) 56
Armaan Mann (9) 57

Ruislip Gardens Primary School, Ruislip

Alisha Ubhi (10) 58
Elena Lewis (10) 59
Megan Quirk (10) 60
Supriya Thapa (10) 61
Kara Pengelly (10) 62
Dylan Surridge (9) 63
Tyla Watson (10) 64
Daniel Morley (10) 65
Kalina Bwalya (10) 66
Isabel Immanuwel (10) 67
Matteo Shirley (10) 68
Lily Freeman (10) 69
Bayley Buckley (9) 70
Hannah Pengelly (10) 71
Chase Devereux (10) 72
Alina Limbu (10) 73
Efrem Mussie (10) 74
William Greenwood (10) 75
Nicholas Tebbutt (10) 76
Callum White (10) 77
Ava Embleton (10) 78

St John's Beaumont School, Old Windsor

Arjan Lai-Kar (10) 79
Rufus Dangerfield (11) 80
Felix Burnham (10) 81
Olivier Gauthier (10) 82
Neal Khullar (10) 83
Tommy Madoc-Jones (9) 84
Michalis Papadopoulos (10) 85
Zavier Knight (10) 86
Enrique Palicio Portus (10) 87
Rufus Gould (10) 88
James Tompkins (10) 89
Shaurya Gupta (10) 90
Alex Bobs (10) 91
Liam Kanaan (10) 92
Yuvvraj Grewal (10) 93
Adwit Sharma (10) 94
Eashar Sandhu (10) 95
Dominic O'Brien (10) 96
Damir Shestakov (10) 97
Reuel Johnston (10) 98
Tom Mylchreest (10) 99
Sean Zheng (9) 100
Sajan Singh Brar (10) 101
Joaquin Borekull Urrutia (10) 102
Ethan McDonald (10) 103
Harrison Terrington 104

St Richard Reynolds Catholic College, Twickenham

Milo Ketteringham (9) 105
Finbar Harris (9) 106
Yudayan Naidu (9) 107
Sienna Minhas (8) 108
Bosley Brown (9) 109
Nikola Nycz (9) 110
Emeline Gee (9) 111
Miguel Mendoza (9) 112

Anne-Marie Kostov (8)   113
Liza Coimbra (9)   114
Ethan Nicol (8)   115
Aleksander Slodkiewicz (9)   116
Euan John Fitzgerald-Monk (9)   117

Streatley CE Primary School, Streatley

Eleanor Nancy Bowers (8)   118
Emily Chadwick (8)   119
Lucia Kennedy (9)   120
Ariana Jessica Kernan (8)   121
Roscoe Hanson (9)   122
Isla Josie Sexton (8)   123
Patrick Dineen (8)   124
Felicity Drage (9)   125
Lily Harrow (8)   126

The Hill Primary School, Caversham

Amelia Webster (10)   127
Jensen Ellmer (10)   128
Fraser Charlie James   129
Harrison (10)
Ella Matthews (10)   130
Charlie Green (9)   131
Jacob Pimm (10)   132
Mia Eggleton (10)   133
Helen Argyropoulou (10)   134
Elsa Patterson (10)   135
Hadiyah Zaman (10)   136
Isaac Ford (10)   137
Dylan Wilson (9)   138
Lilac Ivey-Michie (10)   139
Alex McAndrew (9)   140
Edward Waters (10)   141
Rupert Tollet (10)   142
Ali Hussaini (10)   143
Alice Clifford (9)   144
Imogen Herbert (10)   145

Juniper King (10)   146
Caterina Demiris (10)   147
Ben Attwood-Brown (10)   148
Riley Chandler (10)   149
Saadiq Alikhan (10)   150
Zara Jamal (10)   151
Ayman Adam (10)   152
Fynn Sebastian Sturk (10)   153
Ruby Riddington (10)   154
Luca Elliot Bundy (10)   155
Sydney Layla Grant (10)   156
Josh Glister (10)   157
Charlie Harvey (9)   158
Chloe Gritten (9)   159

Trevelyan Middle School, Windsor

Cameron Maskell (11)   160
Ehsan Chandhar (10)   161
Katie Fry (10)   162
Isaac Jansen (11)   163
Sydnie Maclaughlin (10)   164
Kitty Warren (10)   165
Delphi Perkins (11)   166
Oliver Comley (10)   167
Lybah Hussain (10)   168
Willem Max Murphy (10)   169
Tom Crossland (10)   170
Grace Anne Clarke (11)   171
Ibrahim Niaz (11)   172
Poppy Warren (10)   173
Marissa Gaynor (11)   174
Bronwen Crick (11)   175
Omory Samms (9)   176
Freddie Burchell (10)   177
Charlie Burlison (11)   178
Cassius Wise (10)   179

Western House Academy, Cippenham

Jaylin Boubker (9)	180
Aaisha Giri (8)	181

Willow Tree Primary School, Northolt

Dawand Sirwan Jamal Rashid (10)	182
Anjali Kumar (11)	183
Ali Shidane (11)	184
Iman Yassaa (10)	185
Nelly Siddiqi (10)	186
Nojus Arminas (10)	187
Robert Bunker (10)	188
Maryam Baloch (10)	189
Faizan Arshad (10)	190
Stephen Pavel Thomas (10)	191
Adiyta Kumar (8)	192
Clara Craciun (8)	193
Jeshan Jegatheeswaran (9)	194
Dominik Sebastian Adamczyk (9)	195

THE
MINI SAGAS

World War I Football

Bang! The tank blasted.

"It's Christmas, hooray! No war at Christmas!" I woke everyone up and we ate breakfast. We went outside.

"Oi, UK? Wanna football match?" bellowed a German in a very German accent.

"Fine!" we yelled as I retrieved a football. We played. I was a star striker. I dodged past the German players, slid under the legs. Soon, the score was five-five. Only one minute left. I snatched the ball of a German, tackling another. Three... two... one... I scored! Later, we celebrated. I won a prize off of the Germans. Guess what it was? A tank!

Amelia Campbell (9)
Buxlow Preparatory School, Wembley

Horrible Henry!

"Oh, what a beautiful portrait. I order you to tell the Cleves woman to come and marry me now!"
"I have come to see his majesty, Henry, and I also believe he wants me to marry him," commented Anne.
"Oh, yes he does!" called the servant aloud.
"She is very ugly!" shrieked Henry. "I hate that woman!" he kept saying. Then he married Katherine.
When he found out she had a boyfriend, he yelled, "She has a boyfriend! Behead her now!"
Then she was beheaded, so why did Henry just divorce the pretty, good Anne?

Noor Al-Zahra Al-Saraj (9)
Buxlow Preparatory School, Wembley

The Unfair Pharaoh Abraxas

Abraxas, the son of an Egyptian pharaoh, had just heard that Mother and Father had died. They had drowned in the Nile. At this, Abraxas was flabbergasted. He was just wishing for the day to come but he never knew when. As soon as he became pharaoh, he'd punish people if they didn't give him all their toys. He even killed a man who didn't have any toys! The Egyptian people decided they'd had enough of Abraxas, executed him and made his sister, Asia, Pharaoh. Asia ruled fairly and kindly. Every Egyptian was extremely proud of her.

Piera Corinne Telfer (10)
Buxlow Preparatory School, Wembley

The Massacre

Jack was a Celtic warrior. He'd fought in many battles. This was the most petrifying fight. The beastly Romans approached Jack and the other ferocious, bloodthirsty Celts. The fight began instantly. Blood gushed from the bodies, dazzling on the sunlit grass. Ear-splitting screams were heard everywhere. *By the end, everyone will surely be covered in blood*, Jack thought. Suddenly, Jack was pinned to the ground by a Roman with a gleaming silver helmet covered with blood-red horsehair! He wore armour that glittered in the sunlight. He asked what Jack's secrets were. Jack did not tell him...

Ludo Baring (9)
Caldicott Preparatory School, Farnham Royal

The Egyptian Adventure

Sweat poured down my elegant face. The sun glistened brightly. The sky's blueness nearly blinded my eyes. I wandered into a pyramid through the dark entrance. There was nothing but pitch-blackness. I tried to guide myself through the long, winding catacombs. There was a light shining brightly through a keyhole. I thought I was seeing illusions and rubbed my eyes, but it was still there. I tried pushing some bricks around the keyhole. The door opened! I almost fell over myself in astonishment. The sight that appeared before my eyes was nearly too hard to believe! An ancient Egyptian tomb...

Anand Nambiar (9)
Caldicott Preparatory School, Farnham Royal

The Timdon

One morning on the ancient island of Crete, Setheus was in the royal hall with Termeus. A messenger arrived. Setheus scurried to the door. He opened the letter and learnt that the mythical beast, the Timdon, was eating all the fishermen! Setheus and Termeus armoured up ready to battle. They took some horses to the battle.

When they arrived, the boisterous noise of the Timdon could be heard. The monster rose out of the water, its bloodshot eyes staring at them. The monster smeared them with toxic breath! Heroically, Setheus jumped in the air and sliced the Timdon's head off!

Leo Lane Fox (9)
Caldicott Preparatory School, Farnham Royal

The Stadium

I was standing outside the colossal Greek Olympic stadium. As I walked inside, I was flabbergasted to see how massive the stadium was! The roaring crowd was ear-splitting and the chariots whizzed past me! Then suddenly, a guard spotted me with a knife because I'd had my gladiator fighting before and we were killing people so there was real blood on it! They came closer to me. I started to run but I tripped and then they caught me and threw me onto the chariot track. A chariot came racing towards me...

Ludo Manley (9)
Caldicott Preparatory School, Farnham Royal

King Charles II

There was once a king called Charles. He was having a stroll in the forest, then he heard the rustle of leaves. The king's eyes started to turn red. His arms had giant goosebumps.

He said in a wary voice, "Is anyone there?"

Nothing answered back. He tried it again. At that moment, he heard an ear-piercing scream.

He ran as fast as a cheetah to his precious castle and shouted, "Guards, there is this thing in the forest!" But not one guard could be seen...

Charlie Boardman (9)

Caldicott Preparatory School, Farnham Royal

Mr VK's Great Adventure

On a dark, eerie winter's night, the wind howled in the massive mountains of Norway. There lived a Viking as old as a tree who always thought of going to the ancient cave of Norway.

Days passed as the Viking became older and older. Every day, the Viking walked and walked towards the colossal, ancient cave. When he had finally reached the cave, in the blink of an eye, the magical cave lit up as bright as the shimmering, shining sun. This meant the Viking had found his true home!

Agastya Asnani (9)
Caldicott Preparatory School, Farnham Royal

The Runaway

In ancient Rome, there was a servant who was sad and hesitated every day. He thought he could run away from Rome in the night...

The evil emperor was after him. He ran faster than a dog, faster than a deer but not faster than a horse... He was captured and had to walk back to ancient Rome. He was given a choice - he could either work as a servant or live in the dirty dungeons. The servant chose to be a servant for the rest of his life. He was a servant till the day he died.

Alex Lynch (9)
Caldicott Preparatory School, Farnham Royal

The Mummy Awakes

Once, in the shadows of Cairo, lived a tomb robber. He was hungry for money and jewels. He created a cunning plan to rob a tomb at midnight. He had found a tomb in the day, he would now rob the tomb.

He was climbing up the side wall when suddenly, a hole broke in the tomb wall. He peered in. The gold was blinding in his eyes but he had no time to waste. He scrambled in, then he heard a creak. A mummy jumped out behind him and chased him right into the dusty sarcophagus...

Charlie Kane (9)
Caldicott Preparatory School, Farnham Royal

A Mysterious Day Out!

On my rollercoaster journey to ancient Greece, after visiting the Theatre of Epidaurus, there was a twist, an escape throughout my excursion. Bafflingly, a pyramid appeared in the vicinity. My heart was pounding, with fear overwhelming my body. Was I in ancient Egypt or Greece? I found a slender slit inside the pyramid. Inquisitively, I went inside and discovered Pharaoh and mummies were having a bath in the Colosseum. I joined them to unwind later for a lavish dinner. I took a selfie with them and slept inside Castel Sant'Angelo. What a phenomenal experience! Three eras in one trip.

Fudail Ghouri (9)
Cranford Primary School, Cranford

Within A Blink They Were Gone

Every inch and every centimetre was covered in buboes that everyone dreaded to touch. Our temperatures increased by the minute and the contagious disease had no mercy. The buboes ranged from as small as a pebble to as large as an orange. Our bodies had little understanding of what was going on, they would be dripping in sweat, yet still shivering. God was not awakening to our prayers and the doctors were as clueless as we were. I sent almost everyone I knew to their grave. This unforgiving disease snatched everything from me. My friends, family, everything...

Aiza Butt (10)
Cranford Primary School, Cranford

The Three-Headed Monster

Water dripped from the rough ceiling of the tower as Perseus advanced through the castle. His hand trembled, but he headed on to face his enemy. Finally, he reached the Chimera. Its eyes were red slits. Suddenly, it gave an ear-splitting roar. Fire rushed through the Chimera's mouth as it lit up the dark cave, nearly engulfing Perseus in flames. He ran around and, within seconds, he had thrust his sword into the Chimera's heart. Poison gushed from its body. Roaring in anger, it fell to the ground. Perseus was triumphant. The Chimera was dead.

Abdul Rahman (10)
Cranford Primary School, Cranford

Perseus' Quest

One glistening day, Perseus had a mission to go and kill a hideous beast called Medusa. Medusa was cursed by Athena, goddess of war and wisdom. Hermes gave Perseus winged sandals so he could fly and Athena gave him a polished shield. Hades, god of the underworld, gave Perseus a helmet of darkness so he could go invisible, while Zeus gave him a shimmering sword. Perseus sailed to Medusa so he could kill her. While Perseus was fighting, he tried not to look into Medusa's eyes. He used his shield and she turned to stone. Perseus cut off her head!

Enrol Lobo (9)
Cranford Primary School, Cranford

He's Coming

Outside, the howling of men would be all you could hear at the time. Dust blew into my face and, although I was allergic to dust, I had to keep quiet. My heart was pounding out of my chest, but silently, as quiet as it could. You could hear the spears going through the bodies of men in the dead silence of my hiding spot. You could hear the breathing of the king, King Arthur. Athena, choosing who died or survived, made a bad choice to let King Arthur win. The worst. Wait, here he comes, he's coming! King Arthur...

Atif Shabbir (10)
Cranford Primary School, Cranford

The Olympics... The Beginning

It was dusk as I was walking home down Mount Olympus with a flaming torch to light my way. The path was rocky. I stumbled. The strap on my sandal cut into my foot. I thought it couldn't get worse, but it did... a ferocious, hungry-eyed Chimera swooped down. I ran and leapt behind a rock. Its sharp claws scratched my back and drew blood. I grasped a rock and threw it, striking its head and dazing it. I ran as fast as I could. I reached the village. I found a spear, leant back and threw it...

Fabio Paul-Cruz (10)
Cranford Primary School, Cranford

The Power Of Words

"Here are your scripts for Antony and Cleopatra," declared Shakespeare, handing out scrolls to the King's Men theatre group, "the first part is set in the marketplace where Antony gives a speech over the dead Caesar."

Then, as the words stirred around the theatre like ballerinas darting across the stage, the image of William faded! The King's Men blinked in disbelief. Surely they weren't... A swirling sandstorm toppled over them. Pyramids stood in the background.

They were in ancient Egypt! Palaces stood nearby with columns decorated in hieroglyphics. Shakespeare's script had been powerful enough to send them back there...

Molly Webster (8)
Crazies Hill CE Primary School, Wargrave

The Last Song Of Atlantis

Atlantis was not exactly a merry place. First of all, they were ravenous. Their war with Athens had driven all the fish away. Would they perish? They sent a team of their best fishermen to try and get some food. They didn't return. Atlantis was already losing the war but this was just ridiculous! All they could do was hope they wouldn't starve. They thought they were probably done for already. Soon, the Athenians won and banished them to the bottom of the sea. They slowly dropped like a sinking stone and for all anyone knows, they're still there today...

Dexter Varrall (7)
Crazies Hill CE Primary School, Wargrave

The Deaths Of The Romanovs

Anastasia was there with Alexei and Rasputin, sobbing and writing in her diary, trying not to get too upset again. Alexei was just looking at a photo of his family when, unexpectedly, there was a knock at the door. He suddenly sprang to his feet. He heard the door creeping open and there were four quick flashes of white. He recognised them! Alexei screamed and Anastasia ran in to comfort her brother. Rasputin followed Anastasia and asked what the matter was. Alexei said he'd seen the ghosts of their family! They agreed it was the Romanov family and were delighted!

Ruby Skaanild (8)
Crazies Hill CE Primary School, Wargrave

Susie's Trip To Troy

Susie Luck went to Troy to find out some more facts about the Trojan War. She had arranged to meet a 100-year-old man whose name was Hector. He was one of the knights who'd survived the Trojan War.

At last, she arrived in Troy. She could see the beautiful buildings that surrounded her. Hector said he would meet her there. After she'd gone to a shop and got food, Hector showed her the Trojan horse and she even got to go inside! The inside smelt like a smelly sock!

Afterwards, she went back home.

Rosa Jean Mullins (8)
Crazies Hill CE Primary School, Wargrave

The Russian Revolt

About 100 years ago in Russia, I was writing in my diary, then I heard something. I had to stop writing because it was Alexei screaming with pain! I ran through about 200 rooms before finally finding him. He bled ferociously with ruby-red blood pouring out. I screamed for Mum and Dad.

In the end, they came and called Rasputin straight away. He arrived seconds later. When he came, he tried but too much blood came out and Alexei passed away. My heart skipped a beat. My eyes closed slowly. It felt like it was the end of me too...

Cece Giret (8)
Crazies Hill CE Primary School, Wargrave

Anastasia And Alexei

I was dancing with my family, then everyone except me and Alexei disappeared. There was knocking at the door. We ran and ran but they caught up and tightly tied us up.

When I woke up, there was blood everywhere. I thought my brother was dead! I still had hope as I heard footsteps. I was shivering as I heard special spirits - my dead family! Then I heard Alexei. He was alive! I broke free from the cage, ran to him and opened the cage he was in. We were finally free! I hugged him. We ran and ran...

Gweneira Green (7)
Crazies Hill CE Primary School, Wargrave

Anastasia's Life

I'm Anastasia. My family were executed but me and my brother, Alexei, escaped and we went to my friend, the monk Rasputin. He cured my brother every time he bled. Then we ran for our lives. Rasputin was scary so people tried poisoning and shooting him but he did not die! He protected us. We had to pretend to be normal people. It was hard. We tried to tell people but they wouldn't listen. Finally, we were crowned King and Queen of Russia and Rasputin was wrapped in a carpet and thrown into the icy cold river...

Lorelei Southwell (8)
Crazies Hill CE Primary School, Wargrave

Richard II

Once, there were peasants and they were poor so they went to go and see King Richard II. He felt sorry for them and gave them some money. They went to buy some things for themselves. They bought horses to take them anywhere so they would not have to walk to King Richard.
They went back to the king. King Richard gave them some more money and said every Monday, he would give them £10,000 and some shopping. Finally, they bought some new shoes and had a lovely day and lived happily ever after!

Emily Markham (7)
Crazies Hill CE Primary School, Wargrave

The Horrible Battle Of Bosworth

I am Richard III. I was King of England, but all was not peaceful. The Battle of Bosworth was happening! A man sadly burst through the door (this is Henry Tudor I'm talking about).

Then he said, "Where is he? Where is Richard? I am going to find him and when I do, he won't be alive because he will be stabbed in the head and killed!"

Then he did it and shot me. I was feeling horrible and sick and slept.

Finally, I woke up but still felt horrible, then I fell, dead.

Harry Wetherell (8)
Crazies Hill CE Primary School, Wargrave

Revenge!

The Kingdom of Troy was a very powerful city and greedily stole ships' cargo and brought it to Troy. The sailors wanted revenge. Not long after, they had a plan to build a wooden horse because that was their only way into the gates of Troy. Then they would get their revenge!
As soon as they finished the horse, they went to Troy and the people of Troy thought it was a gift from Athena. They brought it in to Troy, then celebrated but the people inside soon burnt the city...

Dexter Reynolds (7)
Crazies Hill CE Primary School, Wargrave

The Mummies Destroy Egypt

One shimmering day in Egypt, an enormous tornado strategised and started howling and shrieking through the cyan airspace. Out of the tornado gambled millions of mummies. This hurricane had manufactured the mummies! All through the day, they demolished the patrimony such as the pyramids, solid statues of pitch-black cats, the valuable jewellery which was stored somewhere restricted and more. The humans living there were not expecting this and were petrified. Soon, a herd of people congregated and one of them was an intelligent tourist. He enumerated a way to solve the predicament. Eventually, Egypt was extricated!

Asmitha Kunaratham (9)
Grange Park Junior School, Hayes

As The Dead Come Back Alive

The Roman had to battle today, but one of his cruel teammates betrayed him in the battle. He came with an acclamation of mummies attacking him. The Roman gasped in fright. Suddenly, the other team surrounded him. He died sadly.
The league surrounded the inanimate crew and said, "Dead man, dead man, come back alive!" They prayed to their infinite god to help a good man come back alive. Would he ever come back?
Years later, pirates came to find treasure and he was under it... Would they die the way the mummies and Romans did?

Ashvin Radha Krishnan (9)
Grange Park Junior School, Hayes

The Ancient Egyptians

One sunny day, a brave hunter uncovered a Brobdingnagian pyramid. The hunter was so anxious that he wanted to see what was inside. As he was walking towards the tomb, it creaked open. So, he went inside. As he was hiking, he saw a box, so he looked around it. The hunter was so curious, he wanted to see what was inside. He opened it and, suddenly, out popped a mummy! As soon as it came out, it chased the hunter rapidly, but then the hunter made a spike trap and ran outside. Then the mummy died.

Anusan Radhakrishnan (9)
Grange Park Junior School, Hayes

Atrocious Air Raids

"Wake up, Matilda!" whispered Mum. I could hear the sirens before my eyes had properly opened. It was the fourth time this week we'd stumbled into our air-raid shelter. I hated this war. I hated everything about it. I pulled on my itchy dressing gown and threadbare slippers and flew down the stairs.

"Wait!" I shouted over the noise. "Teddy!"

"Too late!" screamed Mum. "We have to go now! They're coming!" We stayed in the shelter until morning. Then, I found Teddy. He was sitting upright on top of the pile of rubble that used to be our house.

Willow McGuinness (10)
Hampton Hill Junior School, Hampton Hill

The Death Escape

Bang! Suddenly, as the cold wind whistled and howled, the weak pebbles started to crumble, the Earth started to shake and twist and twirl. The bodies of the dead started to rise. Millie felt a cold drip crawl across her spine. She was trembling with fear.

Crash! Everything stopped. Millie was relieved until she heard some footsteps and creaking of doors. All she did was run for her life, her hands were clutched so tight. She sprinted for her life. She could hear banging like big sticks with a deep voice.

"Argh!" she screamed. It was a caveman!

Elyssa Ahmed (9)
Hampton Hill Junior School, Hampton Hill

Mummifying

"The pharaoh is dead!" screamed the people. He was rushed to the pyramid and there it began, the mummifying process. First, they announced the death. Next, they embalmed the body with sticky oil like glue. Thirdly, they removed the brain and, after that, they removed all internal organs and put them in canopic jars. Next, they dried out the body and wrapped the body from head to toe. Finally, their belongings were placed in the tomb and left for the spirits to catch them. Did you know ancient Egyptians believed that if your name was forgotten, you wouldn't live on?

Tilly Banks (9)
Hampton Hill Junior School, Hampton Hill

The New Viking

Climbing into the longboat, Anglo-Saxon Alvilda didn't know how hard rowing a Viking longboat would be. Alvilda was sneaking into a Viking longboat because she wanted to be a Viking and get away from the Anglo-Saxons.

The next day, the Vikings were going into battle. They were about to lose when, suddenly, Alvilda shot out of a barrel and saved the leader from death. "We won!" cried Alvilda!

"Hooray!" shouted the captain and teammates. They discovered she was a girl, but, because she helped them win, they let her be a Viking!

Skyla Washington (8)
Hampton Hill Junior School, Hampton Hill

The Mummy Who's Afraid Of The Dark!

One stormy night, Lola the Mummy was getting ready, putting on her bandage onesie and her eye mask while her mummy read a book with hieroglyphs called 'The Three Little Pyramids'.

Then a humongous gust of wind appeared from nowhere and her favourite candle went out. Lola was really scared.

Luckily, her mummy came and helped her look for it. A couple of minutes later, they found it and put it back on.

Next time, she would keep the flint in a secret, special place and remember where it was so that she was ready.

Amber Howard (9)
Hampton Hill Junior School, Hampton Hill

Done And Dusted

Mark Anthony and Julius Caesar were fighting in front of Cleopatra about who got to marry her. She invented a task they both had to complete to win her heart. The first one to reach the top of the pyramid would get to marry her.

The men started running but neither of them reached the top, they both fainted halfway and rolled back down, covered in sweat, sand and bumps. Cleopatra widened her eyes in shock and disappointment. Her jaw dropped. She mumbled to herself, "Well, so much for a happy ending. Those are done and dusted!"

Helena Meyer (10)
Hampton Hill Junior School, Hampton Hill

The Great Escape

It was a hot, sunny afternoon in Pompeii. Cecilia worked on a street stall selling tunics. She liked to watch the big mountain from where she worked. Suddenly, she heard a loud rumble and felt the ground shake beneath her feet. She looked up at the mountain and saw fire spit and a huge plume of smoke! The mountain was actually a huge volcano and it was erupting! She dropped everything and ran as fast as her legs would carry her to the beach. She jumped in a fishing boat just as the eruption buried Pompeii behind her...

Lara James (8)
Hampton Hill Junior School, Hampton Hill

Time Flies With You Mummy

Crash! Bang! Wallop! I skidded to a halt on the banks of the muddy River Nile in my time machine. I popped my head out and saw a giant pyramid above me. Inside, I was greeted by a petrifying mummy. From the right-hand side of the sky came a scorpion. He squirted poison into the mummy's mouth. I leapt and pulled out the poison from the mummy's mouth to save her life. We became friends and got in my time machine. We went back to HHJS where the mummy became the best history teacher in the world!

Olivia Morgan (8)
Hampton Hill Junior School, Hampton Hill

The Red Cross

The sun smiled down on London. Claire was doing her daily errands when there was a heavy, devastated sigh.

"Sir, what's wrong?" questioned Claire.

"Oh, it's none of your business, you nosy brat!" screamed Master Bill.

"Come here," whispered Hetty.

"What's wrong with Master Bill?" questioned Claire.

"His brother died from the plague."

"What's the plague?" asked Claire.

"It's a nasty disease caused by filthy animals like cats and dogs," replied Hetty.

Suddenly, there was a sharp rap on the door and then the chains clinked.

"Lord have mercy upon us!" said a dull voice.

Misha Gambhir (10)
Orley Farm School, Harrow On The Hill

The Magnificent Moon Landing

1969, a year of triumph, when man did the impossible. 20th July, 1969, and astronauts Neil Armstrong, Buzz Aldrin and Michael Collins were going on a historic journey, Apollo 11. Mission Control, as you'd probably expect, was bustling. Final checks were in progress by the most skilled computer scientists, one of which was Margaret Hamilton.

One hour before lift-off, at 8:32, the astronauts making history anxiously walked over to the launch pad. Standing proudly was their rocket, Saturn V. Standing at 110m, it was the tallest rocket ever! Ten! Nine! Eight! Seven! Six! Five! Four! Three! Two! One! Blast off...!

Nerisa Patel (10)
Orley Farm School, Harrow On The Hill

Alone

Lilly walked down the lane, looking at the doors, the red cross all over. Lilly ran back home in case she got the plague.

"Hello, Mother. Hello, Father!"

"Good evening, Lilly!" said Lilly's mother.

"I, I feel feverish..." said Lilly's father.

"What?" exclaimed Lilly.

He went to bed and then they called the plague doctor but, when he got there, Lilly's father was dead from the plague. Her house was marked as a plague house, her worst fear.

The next day, her mother died. The last person alive, alone, was Lilly. She was the only survivor.

Katie Bone (10)
Orley Farm School, Harrow On The Hill

Lord Have Mercy Upon Us

The sun sprayed London with sunshine as Mary was busy doing her chores. Her mum and dad were talking to each other and, even though she knew it was bad, she eavesdropped and they were saying something about a 'plague'. She was so confused. Her mum said something about her friends, they started dying.

"Go back to doing your chores!" her mum suddenly bellowed. They hated her until, one day, Mary suddenly died. Mary's mum and dad were in mourning, even though they hated her. They regretted it now and wished they hadn't shouted at her, they regretted it all.

Aleena Parkar (10)
Orley Farm School, Harrow On The Hill

The Rat-Catcher Of London

Yet again, another died in the hands of Constance Ringington. Weeping, she made her way to the inn called Ye Olde Henry VIII Inn. She ordered a beer and started, once again, making more hopeless medicine to try and cure the bubonic misery. However, a young, handsome lad came in. He sat down with Constance. They negotiated. After a while, Constance finally said, "Are you sure you can cure the Foul Death of the Ingles?"
"Yes," Tommy replied.
Later that day, Tommy led the rats to Gascony using his flute. The mayor gifted him Tommy Kemp Bridge.

Oskar Robb (10)
Orley Farm School, Harrow On The Hill

Darren's Plague Disaster

One fine morning in the bright country of England, there was a boy called Darren. He was a tall, scruffy boy. There was a disease going around, it was called the plague. Darren lived with his master in a queer, ramshackle house.

One day, Darren's master was ill. Darren screamed and cried. Then a few guards came and locked up the door, the windows, everything and put a red cross on the door and wrote, 'Lord have mercy upon us'. All cats and dogs were killed, they thought they gave you the plague. But Darren's prized possession was Scruffo...

Krishna Sriram (10)
Orley Farm School, Harrow On The Hill

The Hidden Killer

My brother died yesterday and was taken to a mass grave pit. We ran out of the house, tears on our faces running like rivers down our cheeks. We saw them put the cross on the door.
"Smell this tobacco, I'll get a wagon."
When he came back, we decided to pay the wagon man all our money. We went to Salisbury, deciding to follow the king. Seven thousand people died and we wanted to live in an area with few deaths and clean air. Something then happened which froze our blood and drenched us in dread. We all had fevers...

Tej Pandey (10)
Orley Farm School, Harrow On The Hill

A Red Cross

Tom and Ben were walking down the empty streets of London, talking about the Plague when, all of a sudden, Ben started coughing violently. He vomited and sweated and couldn't see properly. Tom thought he had the plague as, the past week, seven thousand people had died of the deathly Plague. What was Tom meant to do? It was nearly 9pm and Tom had to go in.

The next day, Ben had died and Tom knew that because there was a red cross on the door where he lived and there was a message saying 'Lord have mercy upon us'.

Khushali Pattni (10)
Orley Farm School, Harrow On The Hill

The Plague

It was a beautiful day. Me, Emily and Bill were walking to school, scared, terrified. We kept walking, worry building up inside us every time we heard the bells or saw a red cross on a door. The word hit me hard every time I saw the words 'Lord have mercy upon us'. As I walked into class, Hetty was racing towards the wall. She turned around, I jumped. She was... different, something was wrong. I knew what it was: the plague! I quickly gave her my medicine, she needed it. I'm glad she's alive!

Khushi Patel (10)
Orley Farm School, Harrow On The Hill

I Won't Come Out To Plague Today

9th August, 1665. It felt like the hottest day ever. It was the hottest day ever. I was staring and gaping at the sickly sight, all those bodies heaved onto small carts in piles. My friends were outside, slowly dying. I wished I could open the windows and scream, "Come inside!" but it was too late. My eyes were stung with tears and as red as blood. "Curse this horrid Plague!" I was terrified but I realised there were many more horrible events to go through.

Ravin Abhayarickrama (10)
Orley Farm School, Harrow On The Hill

Romzy, Jaque And The Beast

Before your father was even a twinkle in your great, great nan's eye, King Julian had two amazing soldiers in ancient Egypt. One day, he ordered Romzy and Jaque to kill an evil beast who ruled the underworld called Assaultinator.

They trampled through deep caves until finally, they reached the underworld. A shadow awoke from its slumber and a body emerged from the lava. A roar echoed up the walls. Romzy leapt in the air and slashed Assaultinator's stomach, making it leap up, throwing Jaque to the side, nearly killing him. The beast lost all blood. They'd completed the task!

Liam Murphy (10)
Priory School, Slough

Tutankhamun Returns

Olivia and I walked inside the dusty, humid pyramid. Her uncle, the famous archaeologist Mr Clarke, was exploring a new hidden tomb. It was fascinating! As I looked around, I noticed a strange and unusual thing in the wall. I felt curious and slowly touched it. Suddenly, the tomb started shaking. The ground shook like an earthquake and we heard loud rumbling sounds. We all screamed in fear and confusion. Then suddenly, there appeared a mummy! I froze in shock.

The mummy spoke loudly, "I, the great pharaoh Tutankhamun, have returned to Earth to rule Egypt once more..."

Maya Ahmed (8)
Priory School, Slough

Dinosaur Escape

Peter heard the growls of animals in the jungle but then he saw it... It was a dinosaur! Then Peter crept away. "Please don't see me, please!" But then it turned around. "Oh great, it's seen me! Enough skulking, let's just run!" The dinosaur was called Bob and he was hungry! When Peter was running, he tripped! Luckily, he got up. "Phew, that was close!" Then a stampede of slow dinosaurs got in his way. "Come on!" As the scary dinosaur got closer and closer, Peter got more worried. Then he tripped and the dinosaur came beside him...

Peter Veer Jennings (9)
Priory School, Slough

The Afterlife

One day, a pharaoh rose from his coffin to go to the afterlife. But before he could, he had to complete a series of challenges.

He saw his dead sister and she said, "I'll help you." The first challenge was to defeat monsters. Sadly, Amun didn't have the right book to defeat them. Luckily, his sister, Clea, had it! One by one, they defeated the monsters. The next challenge was to see if his heart was lighter than the gods' feather. Luckily, Amun's heart was lighter. They jumped happily together! That was the end of the challenges. Or was it?

Inayah Ashfaq (8)
Priory School, Slough

The Mummy

It was a warm morning in ancient Egypt. The pharaoh and the queen were thirsty so they demanded a drink but the slave forgot to check the pharaoh's drink! As the pharaoh drank the drink, he started to feel dizzy and tired, then he fell! The Egyptian queen was covered with shock. She cried and tried to wake him. A doctor was called in to see him. The pharaoh was pronounced dead from poisoning!

A day after the pharaoh's death, the Egyptian queen was going to add another possession for him in his tomb, but the pharaoh's mummy was gone...

Grace Gealy (9)
Priory School, Slough

A Sacred Gem

Many eons ago in the time of ancient Egypt, all was fine in the city until one day, a pair of time travellers appeared in the centre of the city, not knowing what to do. Meanwhile, a beautiful girl, Alexandria, was strolling around her hometown. This was a very unusual day for her. The magical amulet in her headpiece was glowing! Alexandria came to an end where she met the time travellers, Amelia and Leo. "You're here! Hurry, we need your help defeating Anubis!" they exclaimed.

Together, they set off to the most unusual battle of their lives...

Noemi Ingrid Mistur (11)
Priory School, Slough

Ancient Milothons: Katrina's Year To Shine

The wind howled as Katrina left Ireland. Katrina moved to ancient Milothons to start a new life. Ancient Milothons was in ancient Greece. She wanted to pursue her passion for sports so she joined the Olympics. She travelled many miles to get to Olympia. Suddenly, she was missing her family. She had no idea how to make contact with them! At this point, she was regretting the decision she'd made but she stayed.

The next day at the ancient Olympics, Katrina tried her best. She wanted to please her family. Soon, all of her hard work had paid off!

Fahtima Javed (10)
Priory School, Slough

Dinos - Argh!

I ran and ran, not daring to look back, my heart beating faster than ever. I ran like my life depended on it... because it did!

"Food! Food!" they shouted hysterically like wild animals.

The cavemen chased me, banging their clubs on the walls of the damp cave. Their shouts echoed.

"Go away, I'm not even that tasty!" I said.

All of a sudden, their shouts were replaced by screams of dread then silence. A big thud shook the cave. My heart raced. A shadow began to consume me.

I looked up. *Roar!*

Ghaith Al-Janabi (10)
Priory School, Slough

Gladiator Death Maze

Once, the Roman emperor was bored so he made a maze. The maze was dangerous with traps. He put a wanted criminal in the maze and four gladiators had to hunt him down and the first one to find him would be set free! When the game started, everybody started to shout, "Die, die, die!"
If the gladiators ran into each other, they had to fight to the death. A gladiator was stabbed in the stomach but killed his opponent and killed the most wanted thief! He got 100,000 gold coins for winning and went to hospital and luckily survived!

Armaan Mann (9)
Priory School, Slough

Aphrodite

The storm raged furiously. *Boom!*
"Zeus, help!" Hera cried desperately.
"Alright," bellowed Zeus over the devastating storm as he went to find help. Hera took Hermes and Aphrodite to a tower where no tsunamis were near. Devastated, Zeus swam back to tell everyone the bad news. "I can't find help!" wept Zeus.
Aphrodite decided to take matters into her own hands. She swam through chaos to find Poseidon at the source of the storm.
"Help!" Aphrodite called. Poseidon heard her, turned around, saw Aphrodite and glided towards her. She broke his trident! The water disappeared!

Alisha Ubhi (10)
Ruislip Gardens Primary School, Ruislip

The Beginning Of Dreamtime

The aboriginal girl and her dad walked onto the cliff underneath the glistening rainbow. The girl listened inquisitively, her eyes bulging as her dad talked about Goorialla cutting the land, making gouges and tickling frogs to fill it with water, producing life. He talked about the ravenous rainbow serpent tricking two men into his mouth. The girl listened intently. "*Gulp!* The men were swallowed!" the dad explained theatrically. Afterwards, she heard about how Goorialla fled to the sky and felt for the man's family. "We have this radiant rainbow as an apology from the rainbow serpent..." he told her.

Elena Lewis (10)
Ruislip Gardens Primary School, Ruislip

Off With His Head!

Queen Victoria lay awake in her bed. She woke Prince Albert. "Darling, why did we have nine children? I'm dreading another birthday party..." The guests arrived, Victoria's palace was full of excited children. The entertainer was telling jokes, the children laughed while the adults groaned. The entertainer was building to a grand finish involving a custard pie. The entertainer, keen to please the Queen, moved closer to her. A bump, a trip... to the horror of everyone, the Queen was covered in custard. No one laughed.
"Off with his head!"
The entertainer was never seen again.

Megan Quirk (10)
Ruislip Gardens Primary School, Ruislip

The Secret Door

I meticulously walked towards the door. I heard the faint sound of mum calling, "Dinner time!" However, my thoughts drowned out the voice. I was intrigued; what was behind the door? I came to an abrupt halt. I grasped onto the knob, twisted it and pulled. Suddenly, a blazing, blinding light spewed from the door. Cautiously, I approached the door like a moth drawn to light. Then I was pushed through the door and stumbled over something. Baffled, I nervously lifted my head up and saw a man with a fancy crown. Standing there was Pharaoh Tutankhamun...

Supriya Thapa (10)
Ruislip Gardens Primary School, Ruislip

Board Game

"Woohoo, yeah!" Gleaming with the scales of her tail, Chess, a beautiful dragon with a coat of diamond and a tail of glory, was racing her brother, Checkers. "I told you that I would win!" said the amazing Chess while her obsidian-coated brother was still flapping his glorious wings.
"No fair! I told you like a billion times that your wings are firmer and tail is stronger, so you have an advantage!"
Chess and Checkers may have had differences between each other but one thing they had in common was their fear of Vikings - and there was one right there...

Kara Pengelly (10)
Ruislip Gardens Primary School, Ruislip

Romans Invaded By Dinosaurs

In the centre of Rome, the Romans were living peacefully when, one hot day, they heard some loud shakes coming from the colossal forest nearby. The next thing they saw were two huge dinosaurs coming towards them.

"Roar!" came a loud voice from the dark, shadowy forest.

"Roar!" shouted the other from the broken-down, shadow-like forest.

The Romans called their leader, Steve, and the Romans went to attack. The dinosaurs wiped out the Romans and claimed the huge land. The dinosaurs fought Vikings and Anglo-Saxons and Greeks. They stopped when, sadly, Rex died.

Dylan Surridge (9)
Ruislip Gardens Primary School, Ruislip

The Sandquake

One afternoon, me and the Viking gang came one by one. Suddenly, the ground was shaking. It was thunderous! At that moment, the sand blasted into the air, spinning and turning. The Viking chief unfortunately got swallowed. I bravely jumped in the sky and, randomly, fell back down, gladly. It started to rain because of the cold season. All of the Vikings were laughing. The Viking chief tumbled to the floor looking like he'd broken some bones. "Help me lads!" he said while he suffered. Then I snuck away. The rotten Vikings wondered where I was. What a rotten day!

Tyla Watson (10)
Ruislip Gardens Primary School, Ruislip

The Titans

On the beautiful horizon, the Titans rose from the depths of the ocean. The Titans started to make a place called Greece. After a century, Greece was created, along with eight mighty gods, Zeus, Poseidon, Hades, Hera, Demeter, Chiron and Hestia. The humans were created by Zeus. The mighty Zeus was king of all of the powerful gods. Zeus destroyed a dark phoenix's home and it cursed Zeus and made him evil. Zeus then started to destroy homes and crops of everyone he knew. Zeus's siblings destroyed the phoenix, reversing the curse. Peace was restored to the land.

Daniel Morley (10)
Ruislip Gardens Primary School, Ruislip

Revenge...

The streets of ancient Thebes weren't safe. On the edge of slums was the most dangerous place you could imagine. The bravest of people wouldn't dare to go there. In this place lived a terrible priest. He practised black magic. He was dangerous. On a stormy day, the priest, Arold, was reading his Holy Book, which was as thick as a log, when a thunderbolt hit his house. Red flames were everywhere. In seconds, he was dead.
The next morning, something bad happened. He turned into a mummy. He created havoc. He had one thing to do: destroy Pharaoh Ramses...

Kalina Bwalya (10)
Ruislip Gardens Primary School, Ruislip

Sibling Rivalry

Apollo and Artemis were up on Mount Olympus. They were arguing that the other person's job was easier. Zeus had enough, so he told them to swap roles for a day. At first, they found it easy. Artemis flew past the morning sky in the sun chariot whilst Apollo chilled in his glistening moon chariot. But chaos struck when their paths crossed in the sky. Artemis lost control over the sun, so streets caught on fire. Apollo snoozed off so cities were light when it should have been night. After that fiasco, they realised how tricky their jobs were.

Isabel Immanuwel (10)
Ruislip Gardens Primary School, Ruislip

The Attack

A long time ago in the English countryside, people were farming peacefully. The soldiers were relaxing in the sun. Suddenly, lots of Viking longboats came rushing in. The Vikings dismounted and attacked. They held the farmers hostage. They killed many of the soldiers. The English army was defeated. The news spread to a nearby town and the knights were on their way. They finally reached a hill to shoot their crossbows. Two other soldiers went for close combat. At last, they defeated the Vikings. They got rewarded with lots and lots of riches.

Matteo Shirley (10)
Ruislip Gardens Primary School, Ruislip

The Good Vs The Bad

Five hundred years ago, in Olympus, great and powerful gods and goddesses lived peacefully together. One day, there was a big party and it was very loud. The party attracted the attention of Thanatos, Hypnos, Lyhionos and Hydronos, the four demons of the Underworld. They came to the party and declared war on immortals. They all fought and there were many punches and kicks but the gods triumphed and Zeus, the king of all gods, locked them up in the Underworld once again. To celebrate, they had cake and an even better, bigger, noisier party.

Lily Freeman (10)
Ruislip Gardens Primary School, Ruislip

Praise For Poseidon

As the hot midday sun beat down on his brow, the sweat trickled down his neck. The blisters on his hands began to throb. He was exhausted and his mouth felt as dry as the summer sand. He felt total and utter despair at his situation. Would he ever see his family again? Eventually, he slipped into a peaceful sleep and dreamt of his home and family. Suddenly, Poseidon's strong grip clenched the base of the boat and raised the old, wooden boat. It was transported back home and he woke at home with his family, safe and sound.

Bayley Buckley (9)
Ruislip Gardens Primary School, Ruislip

The Deep End

There was a girl named Emily who loved the sea. One day, Emily went out into the Northern Sea. The bubbles were like glass balls and the water was cold as ice. As Emily swam deeper, she began to touch the sandy sea bed. The seaweed was green as fresh vomit and all around her were brightly-coloured fish. As she swam further, it became dimmer, then something came out from the distance. It had blood-red eyes and fins as sharp as knives! It was the size of two blue whales. It was a megalodon and it was swimming towards her!

Hannah Pengelly (10)
Ruislip Gardens Primary School, Ruislip

The Missing Mummies

One morning, a boy called Alex got dressed and headed out. He was going to Egypt's national museum. He went to go and see the mummies straight away. He was always interested in them because he thought one of his ancestors might be one. He searched on the internet for hours but, when he got to the mummy station, all of them were gone. The police searched everywhere but couldn't find them. He figured that a thief might have taken them and probably sold them. Then, suddenly, he saw one, it was eating something...

Chase Devereux (10)
Ruislip Gardens Primary School, Ruislip

The Mysterious Door

I woke up in my cosy bed and peered around my bedroom. Immediately, I noticed a glowing, mysterious door in the corner of the room. I was so curious to find out where it led. Still wearing my pyjamas, I slowly opened the door. I realised I was in a large pyramid filled with amazing treasure! As I gazed around the chamber full of riches, I noticed an old coffin. I carefully walked over towards it, making sure I wouldn't break anything. Unfortunately, I didn't know there was a mummy inside...

Alina Limbu (10)
Ruislip Gardens Primary School, Ruislip

Mummy Rising From The Dead

One beautiful day, me and my family wanted to go to outstanding, amazing Egypt. When we arrived, there was a massive hotel, but my mum led me to the worst hotel, it was like we were in 1912. At least the good thing was I got to stay up for an hour on my phone.

At midnight, I saw a terrifying, horrible zombie rising from the dead. I went back to my bed and repeated, "This is not real!" I went to get some water. However, I felt panting behind me. I was flabbergasted. It was a mummy!

Efrem Mussie (10)
Ruislip Gardens Primary School, Ruislip

1595 Was A Good Year

I put down a pen and allow myself a big smile. I have finally finished my play. It took so long to finish as there were a lot of twists and turns and even right to the end, I wasn't sure what was going to happen. It is a story about star-crossed lovers which is sure to be a big hit with the queen, although she does prefer my comedies. I only hope it doesn't upset her and get me a stay in the tower. She may prefer a story about fairies... I have a great idea. Where's my pen?

William Greenwood (10)
Ruislip Gardens Primary School, Ruislip

Viking Adventure

Once there was a Viking called Arne, he was so adventurous. He went to explore the wild and saw an abandoned temple. He went through the intriguing entrance and a fun trap because it was a rope over spikes. Arne thought he should go back, but it was a once in a lifetime opportunity, so he did the rope swing trap. Arne came across a lot of treasure after that fun trap. Arne thought, *Be careful!* because you should never be greedy with money. He escaped back home safely.

Nicholas Tebbutt (10)
Ruislip Gardens Primary School, Ruislip

Daedalus And Icarus

One day, Daedalus and Icarus were stuck in a stone prison. It was early morning and Daedalus had the best idea ever. They were going to fly out the window using the pillow material and the wax from the candle to make wings! They were ready to jump out of the window, then they were flying through the air elegantly, apprehensive of what was around them. "Icarus, watch out for the sun..." Daedalus said. Icarus did not listen. Icarus was gone forever.

Callum White (10)
Ruislip Gardens Primary School, Ruislip

The Death On The Cross

On the 19th of April BC, I woke up and realised that I was in the BCs. Everyone was walking with a man named Jesus. So, I went with them.
Six hours later, they were putting up a cross and people were putting nails through Jesus' hands and feet. Then, after they did that, he died and everyone realised that they had killed God, otherwise known as Jesus Christ, the Lord.

Ava Embleton (10)
Ruislip Gardens Primary School, Ruislip

The World

1992. A new world is explored.

"Is it ready to launch?"

"Yes, sir."

Zoom! Up in space!

"Ground Control to COBE, are you okay?"

"Yeah, I'm fine."

"Doesn't look like it..."

"Why?"

"You're heading to Venus!"

"Argh! Ground Control, where should I go?"

"Turn left, then go straight. Sorry, must've dozed off!"

As quick as a flash, COBE headed straight past the Orion Nebula and came across a cloud. It was massive and pushed COBE all around. All COBE could do was go forward and so he did. He lunged forward. He found a majestic planet. Welcome to Planet Hitrae...

Arjan Lai-Kar (10)

St John's Beaumont School, Old Windsor

The Court Of The Gods

It was a tense situation in the court of the gods. Poseidon, Hades, Hercules and Zeus sat in favour of the Greeks. Caesar, Neptune, Apollo and Mars were in favour of the Romans.

"We're here to debate the ownership of Mount Olympus then?" said the judge.

"Indeed!" chimed Poseidon.

"We shall be suing for 127,439 drachmas."

"Noted. Any objections?"

"I object!" replied Neptune.

A collective gasp came from the Viking jurors who instantly scribbled something down. Suddenly, a shower of shards rattled on the rooftop. Now, where Mount Olympus once was, there was just a pile of rubble!

"Jurors dismissed!"

Rufus Dangerfield (11)
St John's Beaumont School, Old Windsor

Romans

The Romans were going into battle against the Carthaginians. The sea was raging and the wind was bashing out against the sails. The cries of the Romans came as they saw the Carthaginians. *Bang!* The first shot rang out. The Carthaginians were enraged.

"Argh!" they cried.

The boats clashed together. *Crash!* The Romans hit the Carthaginians' puny ship again. The water suddenly swooped down overboard. Down the ship went, into the mouth of the sea. The Romans gave a big cheer.

"Hooray!"

The Romans sailed back with the win, having a party with the sails flapping in agreement.

Felix Burnham (10)
St John's Beaumont School, Old Windsor

Viking Crossing

One morning, Vikings from Normandy set off for England across the Channel. As soon as they departed, the winds changed to gale force and they were confronted by rogue waves twenty metres high. But they survived. Eventually, they reached Britain. Their vessel beached upon the shore. England's invasion was happening! The Vikings stole jewellery and slaughtered people. It was a bloodbath never to be forgotten!

Later, in the ninth century, King Alfred came to the throne and defeated the Vikings in battle. By 1066, the Vikings had flocked out of Britain, which lived happily ever after. Or did it?

Olivier Gauthier (10)
St John's Beaumont School, Old Windsor

The Raids

Bloodytooth had been doing the laundry. Then the war came and he was on the boat. The tough mission of raiding would be amazing if they could knock the monks out as it would make it a million times easier!

As the longship reached the land of monasteries, like always, the monks were praying. On Bloodytooth's first time, he'd rampaged like a rhino and now was a legendary Viking. Bloodytooth's armour was unbreakable, especially his solid gold sword.

A few years later, Bloodytooth stole £4,000 but it was his last raid. He experienced a bloody, exhausting, painful death.

Neal Khullar (10)
St John's Beaumont School, Old Windsor

Missing The Lesson

As the leaves dropped, I sat in the same boring classroom that I always had. Then I spotted a ruby-red button under my desk! I pressed it and it took me back to 256BC! Suddenly, I got captured and forced into a legion with 5,000 other people. I managed to survive and got promoted to a guard. I was the queen's favourite!

Then one day, I got speared by a dreadful peasant! I suddenly returned back to my class.

"Where have you been?" shouted the teacher.

"In the toilet," I lied.

"You've missed the whole lesson! You're in trouble..."

Tommy Madoc-Jones (9)
St John's Beaumont School, Old Windsor

Alexander The Great

Before the battle, the Romans were training really hard. Meanwhile, Alexander the Great's sword, shield and spears were getting carefully washed by the miserable slaves. His army were training too, increasing their strength and ability to throw spears hard and fast.

As dawn broke, the battle commenced. Alexander the Great had a disadvantage as he had 200,000 men and Julius Caesar had 400,000 men.

However, Alexander the Great had prayed to the gods to be on his side.

With the help of the gods, he won the battle and was victorious! He had 199,999 men left and Caesar had zero!

Michalis Papadopoulos (10)
St John's Beaumont School, Old Windsor

Gladiator

The gate opened. I slowly walked into the arena, heart pumping, blood rushing. I saw the crowd and at that moment, felt an indescribable feeling. I'd always thought my life was complete but now, something had killed that completeness. It felt like someone had stabbed me in the back... because they had! I fell to the ground, making the dust fly away. Bleeding heavily, I begged my opponent for mercy but he was not fond of the word mercy and said, "There's no mercy!"
I grabbed a rock off the ground and threw it at his head and stabbed him!

Zavier Knight (10)
St John's Beaumont School, Old Windsor

Dead And Lost

The rusty metal palace door creaked. Dry wind entered and two powerful guards set foot in the building holding a fearful slave, a most unfortunate one. Typical.

"What reason do you have to disturb thy queen's peace?" my mother, the queen, asked.

"He is a miserable slave who refuses to work," answered the disgruntled guard for him.

I moaned. I knew he was going to be dead in the blink of an eye! The blade man emerged from the shadows. I couldn't stand it! I put myself in front of the razor-sharp blade... My single whimper was hardly heard.

Enrique Palicio Portus (10)
St John's Beaumont School, Old Windsor

The Coal Mine

The rain bellowed and loose drops swivelled down the drains, flowing like a bath. The two Victorian boys dropped down the coal mine shaft, not keen for any more work. The conditions were dreadful down there with dirt and muck everywhere they stepped. Still, work was needed. The boys were young but still had to work - first, they were pulling and pushing carts.

Later, they had been working for hours, digging, when suddenly, in front of them, stood a proud coal boulder. Scared, they ran but it rolled after them. It was the end! The boys stood face-to-face with darkness...

Rufus Gould (10)
St John's Beaumont School, Old Windsor

The Destination Of Medusa

Trembling in the darkness of the cave, Perseus was terrified. He walked over the cold, damp, murky floor in search of Medusa. The rocks crumbling, his spine tingling, his body shaking, he came across the monster! Blocking his eyes from the sight, he ducked behind his shield and slashed his sword in all directions. In desperate action, he chopped Medusa's head off, blood spitting and splattering in all directions. A piercing scream was in the background. Carefully, he placed the head in his bag, trying not to look at it. He didn't want to be turned to stone!

James Tompkins (10)
St John's Beaumont School, Old Windsor

The Fight Of The Farmers

Beside the deep, twinkling Nile in ancient Egypt, there lived an arrogant farmer named Kamun. When Kamun went to harvest his ripe mangos, Kamun became enraged at the sight of another farmer, whose name was Chungus, uprooting his potatoes. This made Kamun angry. An erupting controversy followed.

Ten minutes later, things were getting out of hand. It was becoming a wrestling match! *Boom!* Kamun pushed Chungus into the Nile! Chungus' screams turned into muffled murmurs as he sank. His last sight was of a pyramid pointing to Osiris...

Shaurya Gupta (10)
St John's Beaumont School, Old Windsor

Gladiator

In Rome, Alex, a gladiator, nervously crept into the majestic Colosseum. The crowd booed and hissed. There was a high sense of peril in the Colosseum. He clenched his sword hard and prepared for the arduous battle he was going to have. Suddenly, as if the gods were angry, a bloodthirsty roar came from behind him and to his horror, there was a gigantic lion!
Alex fought for hours and the audience was hooked. Then the lion pounced, claws out, teeth gleaming, chest forwards... Alex swung his sword frantically. The lion was dead; a hero was born!

Alex Bobs (10)
St John's Beaumont School, Old Windsor

The Raid Of The USA

On a dark, gloomy day, flying over the Pacific Ocean was extremely horrendous and a hard task. Finally, on the brink of the horizon, I saw it - Japan. Every minute, I was getting closer, worrying about misplacing the bomb in the sea. Dropping a 20,000-ton bomb would not be easy, but this was my task and I had to do it for the USA. They were relying on me. As I got close to my destination, I flew towards Hiroshima.

"I'm ready."

Then, at the last moment, I dropped the bomb. A mushroom cloud rose into the white heavens...

Liam Kanaan (10)
St John's Beaumont School, Old Windsor

Landing On The Battlefield

In despair, Yuvvraj, Tim and Fred were about to face one of the deadliest wars of all time. All three of the young men were about to parachute down onto the Normandy beaches where all of the action was happening. Hearts pounding, minds spinning, closing their eyes and hoping for the best, they all jumped out. Drifting slowly down to the battlefield, they all hoped that they would not get shot. Suddenly, a missile hit that killed both Tim and Fred! Straight after, Yuvi was shot in the leg! He lay on the battlefield, not knowing what to do...

Yuvvraj Grewal (10)
St John's Beaumont School, Old Windsor

The Gladiator

I was so nervous. I had never fought a tiger before but being a gladiator, I had to. When I entered the blazing hot and gigantic Colosseum, people looked at me as they never had before. I came face-to-face with the tiger who had been fed nothing for one week just to make the fight more gruesome! It was a hard fight and I got badly wounded on my legs but I finally conquered the tiger! Everyone was clapping for my victory. I was joyous! Suddenly, I was attacked by two very hungry, ferocious and dirty tigers! I died. *Silence.*

Adwit Sharma (10)
St John's Beaumont School, Old Windsor

War In Troy

I was sitting at the gates of Troy with the howling wind slashing against my face. I looked into the distance. I saw a colossal wooden horse rolling towards me! As fast as lightning, I jumped up and sprinted towards the guard.

By the time we came back, the horse had reached the gates so we let it on.

As soon as it entered the city, hundreds of men spilt out of the horse led by Achilles! War had begun. Suddenly, Achilles pulled out a sword and killed Prince Hector. Then I pulled out a poison arrow. *Ping!*

Eashar Sandhu (10)
St John's Beaumont School, Old Windsor

The New Celt Village

Aragon and his tribe clambered over a hill. They saw a village. As they had sailed far across the water, taking this village would be useful. Aragon and his tribe prepared their horses and sharpened their swords. They got all their chariots ready and darted headfirst, slaughtering everyone in sight, blood spitting everywhere. No one was spared, not even children. Aragon emerged victorious and raided all the valuables. His tribe kept the cattle. He was so grateful, he sacrificed his second in command to the gods!

Dominic O'Brien (10)
St John's Beaumont School, Old Windsor

Viking Teleportation

One Monday morning, I was in class reading a Viking book. All of a sudden, I started to teleport to a strange land. Whilst I was teleporting, I saw lots of blue colours. I was really nervous because I didn't really know where I was going. With shock, I had arrived. At first, I thought that I was in a hot country but then I realised that I was in a Viking land! I heard people marching to me and I thought they were normal people. Suddenly, I realised that they were Vikings! I ran into the middle of nowhere...

Damir Shestakov (10)
St John's Beaumont School, Old Windsor

The Death Of Chimera

With the wind blowing against my concentrating face, I rode Pegasus towards my goal - defeating Chimera. Suddenly, I saw its head of a lion, its goat head on his back and its snake-head tail. They were all staring at me! I took a shot with my bow and arrow, and it plonked into its upper thigh. It screamed in pain and shot a fireball. I got an idea. It shot another fireball. I sprinkled gunpowder on my arrow and shot it into its mouth. It caught alight, blew him up and no one was terrorised by him ever again!

Reuel Johnston (10)
St John's Beaumont School, Old Windsor

Deadly Cholera

When I arrived to moor on the River Thames, I could already make out the groaning of the nearly-fallen souls. I stepped off the boat and saw the appalling slumped shapes of flesh and bone begging for food and clean water. I went on further to where I was staying. I could smell the dreaded scent of mould and dirt.

When I arrived at the inn, I immediately stumbled back. I saw dull pictures of Queen Victoria on the wall. I ran back to the boat but I'd been caught but the deadly disease - cholera...

Tom Mylchreest (10)
St John's Beaumont School, Old Windsor

Time Travel Adventure

As soon as it reached 4pm, I rushed out of the classroom. That is when something strange happened... I was in the ancient Egyptian desert and I was a slave! I was to clean the pyramids. I spotted a strange-looking one. I went in and it was full of gold! Suddenly, the Sphinx came alive and chased me. It became faster and faster. As it got closer to me, it reached for me with its claws.
I thought my life had ended but I got teleported home! My mum came and shouted, "Where were you?"

Sean Zheng (9)
St John's Beaumont School, Old Windsor

The Horrors Of D-Day

Trembling, heart racing, me and my comrade, Rob, were shivering on the grey, gloomy boat, waiting for the horrors of war to envelop us. Our boat landed on the blood-red shore that had dead bodies lying on the sand as the clasp of death had grabbed them. I opened the ramp and my comrades stormed the beach gallantly but sooner or later, all fell to the merciless machine gun fire. Suddenly, Rob was screaming. Then his face was obliterated and his voice faded away. Was this really triumph and glory?

Sajan Singh Brar (10)
St John's Beaumont School, Old Windsor

Death Army

I felt my blood spinning as I rang the alarm bell and waited for our army to get ready for the war against the death army. I stood and stared at the army walking slowly, bravely, towards our city, Barcelona. The fierce eyes peered at me as I stood as still as a statue, waiting for my fate. Their shields were red and curved, they had brown sandals and their spears were perfectly made. Our army stood on the frontline, praying to win but one command from Julius Caesar was the end of us...

Joaquin Borekull Urrutia (10)
St John's Beaumont School, Old Windsor

Bad Decision

I had let my village down. I could hear the piercing sound of Tusk with his rotten tentacles as he ripped the back and barricades off my ship. All I could do now was wait till I went up to Valhalla. I, Eric the Third, was supposed to raid an island and defeat Tusk but now I was in a huge problem and I couldn't get out of it. Now my small ship was sinking rapidly. At least I would go down in history... The tentacles were coming up the ship now. I was a complete goner...

Ethan McDonald (10)
St John's Beaumont School, Old Windsor

Ancient Egypt Strikes Again

In the early days of summer, there was a boy who was having an art lesson on ancient Egypt and they were drawing mummies. Suddenly, there was an earthquake! Afterwards, the boy looked down to see bandages wrapping around his limbs. Unexpectedly, he had changed into a mummy! He started biting people and they all turned into mummies. Soon, there were only mummies in the world!

Harrison Terrington

St John's Beaumont School, Old Windsor

Victory On The Victory!

The violent noise of wrecking, destructive cannons smashing ships all over the Atlantic ocean is howling in my ears. I'm on the HMS Victory, it's the 21st October 1805 and we are fighting the French and Spanish navies in the Battle of Trafalgar. I can taste the bitter smoke lingering in the air and the horrid smell of gunpowder wafts around.

Suddenly, there's devastating news. Our heroic Admiral, Lord Nelson, has been shot and is clutching to life. However, there is also good news. We have defeated twenty-two enemy ships and they've retreated. We have won the Battle of Trafalgar!

Milo Ketteringham (9)
St Richard Reynolds Catholic College, Twickenham

The Time-Travelling Diver

Once, there was a time-travelling scuba diver and a petrifying megalodon. The scuba diver travelled to prehistoric times where he discovered the humongous, ancient shark! The megalodon disliked anything around his territory and was raging mad at this stranger who dared to enter his home. The scuba diver was naturally afraid but he was also interested and swam closer. With one massive gulp, the scuba diver was swallowed by the megalodon. He punched, kicked and bit, trying to escape, but the megalodon held on for a while before spitting him out. The scuba diver frantically swam away and escaped.

Finbar Harris (9)
St Richard Reynolds Catholic College, Twickenham

Gideon's Adventure Back In Time!

One day, a boy named Gideon was playing. Suddenly, he fell deep down a sinkhole with gushing wind knocking him. When he landed, he felt something wet and scaly. When he looked around, he was so shocked; there were trees all around and dinosaurs, pterodactyls flying everywhere and many other dinosaurs! Gideon was worried but excited. When he looked at the thing he was sitting on, he knew it was a brontosaurus and it licked his face with a big *whoosh!* Gideon stuck his hand in his pocket and found a chocolate to feed him. That's how they became BFFs.

Yudayan Naidu (9)
St Richard Reynolds Catholic College, Twickenham

The Journey To Rhodes

There was once an adventurous girl who lived in Greece. She was always going on long walks. One day, she decided to go to the castle in Rhodes, it was a day's ride away.

When she arrived, she saw the knight's castle. There were fires burning, lighting the way. It was bigger than she could ever imagine. It had a large, dry moat, massive wooden doors and guards on the towers. She had never seen a knight before, they were dressed in armour with sharp swords. She asked them to play cards. They agreed and it was trumps until dawn.

Sienna Minhas (8)
St Richard Reynolds Catholic College, Twickenham

The Seven Chairs

When all the world was one country, seven Viking elders ruled together and filled the world with peace. But an evil magician wanted to rule for himself. He enchanted each of the elders' chairs to send them away. This caused the world to break into seven pieces and the magician was unable to rule. Since peace no longer filled the planet, the people started to riot against the magician and he was slaughtered. With the magician dead, the enchantment was broken. The seven elders returned and the world was whole and peaceful once again.

Bosley Brown (9)
St Richard Reynolds Catholic College, Twickenham

Escaping Dinosaur

This story started eighty million years ago. It was a nice, sunny morning. My parents sent me to pick blackberries and mushrooms from the forest. When I entered the forest, I started to pick berries into the basket. Behind the tree, I saw a big, moving shadow. I looked closer... it was a T-rex! He saw me and he started running towards me. I left the basket and started sprinting while dodging the trees. I managed to escape by crossing the waterfall. I was safe. I picked up more mushrooms on the way home. It was a really scary day!

Nikola Nycz (9)
St Richard Reynolds Catholic College, Twickenham

The Mummy

People needed to see the body of their dead pharaoh. They wanted to check the remains had not been stolen. The visitors typed in the password and crept in. When they went in, it was cold, damp. Kneeling next to the tomb, they opened it but, to their amazement, the tomb was empty. They all jumped back. They heard noises and then someone saw something stand up. It was a zombie! The mummy had turned into a frightening zombie! One by one, the people turned into zombies and attacked the city until there were no humans in all of Egypt.

Emeline Gee (9)
St Richard Reynolds Catholic College, Twickenham

The Aliens Are Invading

Pebbles tumbled, the ground shook and the strong wind howled. Then a laser beam shone from the sky. My heart froze. I rode on my bike as brisk as I could. The mysterious hovercraft followed me and, before I knew it, trees were floating, animals were floating and other objects. As quick as a flash I realised my bike was also floating. I leapt, hoping I would survive the monstrous invasion.

Then I sprinted as fast as I could to my house. The image of the ship faded in the distance. I realised they were World War Two planes...

Miguel Mendoza (9)
St Richard Reynolds Catholic College, Twickenham

A Girl And Her Older Brother

Long ago, in the Stone Age, there was a girl called Platie and her brother, Joe. They got lost in the woods. Platie ran away in search for help but she got even more lost. She found a little wolf and a bird. She found them near the lake. They looked lost too. They got into her arms. They made her feel better knowing she was not alone. She was very brave so she wasn't really scared. The wolf fell out of her hands! Her brother found them because of all the noise. They finally found their hopeful, kind parents...

Anne-Marie Kostov (8)
St Richard Reynolds Catholic College, Twickenham

Stone Age Dream

In the deep, dark forest, John, James and Kate lived in a cave. They were Stone Age people. They went into the forest searching for food. Suddenly, they heard a terrible roar. It kept getting louder. It was a bear! They ran and ran and then got lost. John was stuck with the grizzly beast. He kept running but saw something odd. There was a shimmer in the distance. John ran and finally got there. His friends suddenly appeared. They went through the shimmery object and teleported into my room. I screamed!

Liza Coimbra (9)
St Richard Reynolds Catholic College, Twickenham

The Wedding

I woke up very excited yesterday! The sun was shining and I was about to get married! Joyfully, I opened the closet door and spotted that my dress was hanging there, so I grabbed it and put it on. Speedily, I got to the lovely castle. I was about to walk down the aisle when the sky darkened and the clouds poured down. A mystery figure stood at the front. I nervously trod down the aisle to find out who I was going to marry. It appeared, to my shock, that my future husband was Henry VIII!

Ethan Nicol (8)
St Richard Reynolds Catholic College, Twickenham

The Aztec Trials To Survive

Mike was just having a walk in the forest. For a few minutes, he got lost. After, he found an Aztec city. He could not believe his own eyes. It was an Aztec city!

Suddenly, everyone stared at him. Then the Aztec priest said, "If you are not one of us, we will sacrifice you!"

Then the warriors and the priest charged after Mike. Mike sprinted out of the forest with the warriors behind him. Finally, he had outrun them and, somehow, he was back at his house.

Aleksander Slodkiewicz (9)
St Richard Reynolds Catholic College, Twickenham

The Ghost Of The Castle

My name is Gerald Fitzgerald and I was sent to the Tower of London for being disrespectful to the king in 1534. He ordered his men to chop my head off and I became a ghost. To get my revenge on the king, I began to break everything in the castle and scare the guards. The king brought in some ghostbusters who trapped me in a ghost cage. I realised I was wrong to damage things, so I said sorry but the guards still wouldn't let me go. I'm still here today.

Euan John Fitzgerald-Monk (9)
St Richard Reynolds Catholic College, Twickenham

Florence Nightingale: The Opposite

"Florence, help Tom. He's injured!"

"Okay General!" Florence checked Tom. "You've broken your leg."

Tom was very worried because Florence wasn't a good nurse and her operations didn't work!

"That hurts!"

"Sorry Tom. I will have to replace your leg."

Splat!

"Argh!"

"There," said Florence, covered in blood, "here is a metal leg. Let's just stitch it on... There."

"Look, Florence, the enemy is retreating."

"Right, Tom, let's get outside. Oh, the Duke's here, injured. The Duke of Cambridge is safe in our hands!"

Later.

"Oh!" said Tom. "Florence is dead! She took arsenic as a cure for her headache!"

Eleanor Nancy Bowers (8)
Streatley CE Primary School, Streatley

Julius Caesar

2,000 years ago, Julius Caesar was a wealthy man. He loved nothing more than gold. He had ten servants.

"Pick the grapes and feed me wine!" he would say.

Brutus was a friend of Julius and was jealous of him. Julius wanted to be king but Brutus didn't approve of this idea.

"Julius?"

"Yes?"

"Maybe it'd be nice to give some money to the poor."

A year later, Julius had lost most of his money and then knew how hard it was to be poor. Now he could become king! He made all the rich people give the poor £10.

Emily Chadwick (8)
Streatley CE Primary School, Streatley

Dinosaur Attack

I was relaxing. I heard rumbling, then the attack began! The bottom of my ship was crushed.
"Oh no!" I screamed, but I shouldn't have.
The stegosaurus turned around and ran at me again. It smashed into my boat. I was sinking!
"Lift me up, Do-do!" I shouted to my pet pterodactyl.
The stegosaurus was coming in for another attack.
Then I realised, the stegosaurus was just lonely!
"Stop!" I screamed.
The stegosaurus stopped.
"I'm called Plate," he said.
"I'm called Pete," I said, "wanna come back to mine?"
"Of course!" he replied.
We sailed back across the lake.

Lucia Kennedy (9)
Streatley CE Primary School, Streatley

The Mystery Of The Missing Necklace

Once in ancient Rome, a girl called Julia was in bed. She woke up and couldn't find her necklace! Julia went out of her house and tried to find it. First, she went to Antony and asked where the necklace was.

Antony said, "I think that I saw Hadrian with it."

"Okay, I'll ask him."

Julia set off to find Hadrian.

When she was there, she shouted, "Hadrian, where are you? Oh, there you are!"

"Here, I found this and wanted to give it back to you."

He gave her back her necklace and Julia walked back home.

Ariana Jessica Kernan (8)
Streatley CE Primary School, Streatley

The Boat That Made History

The year was 1912. The Titanic left. Going across the Atlantic was a dangerous route but in no time, the Titanic was going faster and faster. It hit an iceberg! People were trapped under the deck. The water flooded from corridor to corridor. Lifeboats were being launched.

When all of the lifeboats were launched, the lights went out. Crying stopped as the bow of the ship went underwater. The ship snapped and looking in the water, you could only see the bodies of loved ones.

Finally, another boat took the passengers to America. Now the Titanic is a remembered boat.

Roscoe Hanson (9)
Streatley CE Primary School, Streatley

Families United

In dinosaur times, there were two birds called Tom and Amy and they were going to be parents. After waiting for a long time, their egg hatched. They called the chick Leo. But when Leo's mum and dad went out and left Leo alone, a T-rex came and stole him! But after five minutes, Leo trusted the T-rex who was nice and called Hatty. She had a baby, Sweety. They became a family.

When Leo was two, he went to visit his real family. He told them how fun T-rexes are. Then the two families became one!

Isla Josie Sexton (8)
Streatley CE Primary School, Streatley

The Lost Treasure

Once upon a time, there was a Roman man called
Fig. He was on a quest to find the lost treasure. He
set off along the path to try and find it.
After a long walk, he started to cool off in the dark,
gloomy Dead Sea. He saw the Loch Ness Monster!
He eventually fought it off after five tries. He carried
on swimming and saw a treasure chest ahead. He
unlocked it and inside were jewels galore! He got to
the top of the water. He'd saved the day but he and
the treasure were never seen again...

Patrick Dineen (8)
Streatley CE Primary School, Streatley

The Three Tasks!

In an ancient land called Egypt, there was a kid, Bob, who wanted to be pharaoh. He was told that to be pharaoh, he had to do three tasks. The first task was to go to the tomb of a dancing mummy. "Dance!" said the mummy. "Step on the lit-up tiles." Secondly, he got 100 blocks to build a pyramid. The final task was to prove he would be a good king. Bob's hair was weighed on some scales against a feather. It was lighter. That made him pharaoh! Yes!

Felicity Drage (9)
Streatley CE Primary School, Streatley

The Adventure Made Of Stone

A girl named Dana was in a forest and found a time machine and travelled to the Stone Age! Now she was on a mission to find the magic gem to save the Stone Age village from darkness. Luckily, she had a map. Then she crossed a river which was very hard. The last place she passed was a stone maze which took her an hour to get through.

Finally, she found the gem that was hidden in the maze. She brought it back to the Stone Age village. They could now live in light forever!

Lily Harrow (8)
Streatley CE Primary School, Streatley

Beanie's Mystery Morning

"Beanie, it's your birthday! You're six, a big enough dragon to go out exploring by yourself!"

Beanie skipped off. He got lost and ended up in the middle of the dark, sinister forest. He was just beginning to feel frightened when he heard a friendly voice.

"Hello, I'm Coco."

"Why aren't you called Beanie? Every dragon's called Beanie, like me."

"Don't be silly, dragons have different names!" said Coco.

"Beanie! Where have you been? I've been worried!" called Mum.

"I was talking to my friend, Coco. Oh... Coco's disappeared!"

"Beanie, you're imagining things again! Let's go home for birthday cake!"

Amelia Webster (10)

The Hill Primary School, Caversham

The Vikings

"Ay oh! Ay oh! Ay oh!" shouted the Vikings.

"What should we do?" asked one of the children.

"Hide!" suggested another.

"No!" exclaimed one particularly brave child.

"I say we stand strong and fight; we'll die either way. Are you ready?"

"Yes..." murmured the other children.

"Okay, then let's all march towards the Vikings head-on!" said the brave one.

As the children turned, they saw the Vikings charging up the steep hill to where they were situated. The brave children drove the Vikings mad and eventually, the Vikings all fled back!

Jensen Ellmer (10)
The Hill Primary School, Caversham

Reborn And Not Retired

It was then, that moment when the villains were reborn! Once Hitler, Julius Caesar and Ivan the Terrible had met at Uluru, they knew they wanted to try and eliminate all other humans. They managed to set up a base to plan, so they began discussing ideas.

"We should send an atomic bomb while we watch from space!" suggested Ivan.

"We should slay everyone with our razor-sharp swords!" exclaimed Julius.

"We could burn their houses down! Nah, that's old school!"

"So there we have it, let's drop the bomb!" argued Hitler.

The only question was, would they succeed or fail?

Fraser Charlie James Harrison (10)

The Hill Primary School, Caversham

Run Natalie, Run, Run, Run!

There was no movement, only Natalie who was painting a pyramid. She was standing in the middle of the Egyptian desert whilst painting the pyramid in front of her. As she was getting to the top part of her pyramid painting, the actual pyramid suddenly crashed down. *Boom!* She started running as fast as she could so she wouldn't get squashed. When she thought things couldn't get any worse, mummies started walking in her direction! *They've come back to life!* thought Natalie, still running. A mummy was coming right towards her.
"I'm gonna die!" she screamed, sprinting for her life...

Ella Matthews (10)
The Hill Primary School, Caversham

Splurge!

In the towering cathedral in Rouen, Louis le Rouge watched some knights gingerly squeezing William the Conqueror into his tomb. Louis dreamily thought back to when William was young and tenacious, leading his army to sensational victory at the Battle of Hastings. Years later, William was hunting with Louis when suddenly, a vicious wild boar leapt out of the undergrowth, making William's horse rear in terror. William was pierced by the saddle and later died of an infection.

Splurge! Louis was brought out of his daydream by the putrid smell of the king's guts exploding out of his undersized tomb!

Charlie Green (9)
The Hill Primary School, Caversham

The Mummies Invade!

It was a hot summer's day in ancient Egypt. King Tut had died and Cleopatra was pharaoh. A soldier was guarding King Tut's tomb. He heard moaning from inside. A tall, bandaged figure lurked at the entrance.

"Who's there?" shouted the soldier.

"The end of your race!" cackled a voice.

The soldier was eaten whole! The figure came into the light - a mummy!

A rebellion formed to stop them, as soon there were hundreds of mummies. The rebellion leader, Malsey, went to fight the leader mummy. It was a ferocious battle. Malsey was eaten and mankind hit its deadly end.

Jacob Pimm (10)
The Hill Primary School, Caversham

Cleopatra's Adventure

"I am never going to leave this palace!" I bellowed.
"You have too much power!" Ptolemy exclaimed.
"Yes, because I'm older than you!"
Suddenly, the guards grabbed me. Kicking and screaming furiously, I tried to get out of their painful grasp as tight as a python's grip around its prey. I couldn't escape! I was carelessly tossed into the bustling marketplace. Somehow, I had to get back into the palace to find Caesar! Spotting a carpet stall, I ordered the biggest roll to be sent to the palace. I then squeezed inside before being jolted and carried away...

Mia Eggleton (10)
The Hill Primary School, Caversham

Agor's Birthday Party

A long time ago in the country that we now call Sweden, lived the powerful Vikings. Among them lived a Viking called Agor. You might say that Agor was the biggest, kindest and most harmless Viking of them all. He always helped people and, surprisingly, wasn't vicious and never took part in wars.

On the 29th of June, he woke up and remembered that it was his forty-fifth birthday.

"Happy birthday to me!" he exclaimed.

To his great surprise, when he opened his house door, all his friends chorused, "Happy birthday, Agor!"

Agor hugged them. He was so, so happy!

Helen Argyropoulou (10)
The Hill Primary School, Caversham

The Secret Of The Tomb

"Come on!" shouted Ra from the entrance of the pyramid.

"I'm still not sure whether this tomb is a good idea..." said Cleo, thinking about the rumours she'd heard.

"Come on, let's go!" said Ra, running in.

Cleo followed her brother, shaking with fear and anticipation. Suddenly, there was a rumbling and the door shut behind them, leaving only a sliver of light. Gasping, they turned around to see a figure in the doorway of the next room. It groaned and Ra and Cleo realised it was a mummy! It shuffled towards them and the lights went out...

Elsa Patterson (10)
The Hill Primary School, Caversham

The Divorce

It was a sunny day when King Henry VIII and Catherine of Aragon got married. Catherine became queen, then had a daughter, Mary.
One stormy night, King Henry broke the news to Catherine that he was going to divorce her. At that moment, Catherine's heart broke into a million pieces and crystal clear tears rolled down her face. The next night, they got divorced and there was thunder and lightning outside. Mary was crying her eyes out, wondering what was going to happen next.
After the divorce, Catherine packed up, said goodbye to her daughter and left. Henry moved on...

Hadiyah Zaman (10)
The Hill Primary School, Caversham

Lindisfarne Looters

I was running, sprinting from the chaos and confusion, knowing that anywhere was better than here. I ran faster than I'd even run before, through the expanding sea of people. I was glad that I was smaller than the other monks, this was the reason that I survived. Even the other monks couldn't see good in Vikings. The peaceful monks of Lindisfarne had done nothing wrong to annoy the fearless Vikings. I heard the cries of wounded monks, powerless against the vicious intruders. I looked up to see their longships sailing into the setting sun with our precious relics onboard...

Isaac Ford (10)
The Hill Primary School, Caversham

Anne's Plan

"Anne Boleyn shall be beheaded tomorrow!" announced King Henry VIII.

Anne didn't know about this as she was looking after Elizabeth. Anne's parents sneaked round to the garden and told her everything!

Midnight struck and the plan was carried out. She crept into Henry's room, planning to kill him, but he awoke to a creaking floorboard. Henry leapt up and jumped out of the window onto the wet grass below. Anne followed and all was going well but all this ended when she tripped on a rock and landed in the guillotine! That was the end of Anne Boleyn.

Dylan Wilson (9)
The Hill Primary School, Caversham

Molly And The Ghostly Shadow

Molly loved the Tudors and always told everyone facts about them. When she found out she was going to Hampton Court Palace, she was exhilarated. She couldn't wait to see all the incredible sights! In all her excitement, she lost her parents in the maze and decided to go back to the palace for help. Molly went through an unmarked door to the Silverstick Stairs. She felt a chill down her spine. She instantly recognised the ghost of Jane Seymour standing next to her!
She rushed down to find her parents and said, "You'll never guess who I've just seen!"

Lilac Ivey-Michie (10)
The Hill Primary School, Caversham

The Ultimate Mix-Up

It was the moment they all had been waiting for -
the final battle, Anglo-Saxons against the Vikings.
Harald Hardrada gave the signal. The Vikings
advanced. Harald was just thinking about the
delectable food he'd eat in Norway... that was, if he
won.
The battle began. Swords at the ready, archers
armed, axes ready to be thrown. Just when Harald
thought he'd won, he got caught by Harold
Godwinson! Then William the Conqueror sneaked
up on the two sides and was slaughtering them, not
caring if it was a Saxon, a Viking or even a Norman
soldier! The end was nigh...

Alex McAndrew (9)
The Hill Primary School, Caversham

Vikings Got Talent

His legs trembled with nervousness as he walked onto the stage. Thor, the mighty warrior, destructor of evil, began to sing. As he opened his mouth, the excited audience expected a thunderous roar but to their surprise, a soft, high-pitched sound emerged. The Viking king was singing opera! At first, the crowd giggled and laughed but the beautiful voice soon began to mesmerise them. The power in Thor's voice began to make the walls tremble and before long, the crowd sprung to their feet and began to cheer and clap. The golden buzzer was struck and Thor was the champion!

Edward Waters (10)
The Hill Primary School, Caversham

Are You Sure You Want To Do That, Sir?

On the delicate plains of ancient Egypt, there lived a pharaoh who loved his old relatives dearly but had to kill them because he wanted to be the ruler of Egypt. One day, he went up to his servant and said, "Today, we are going to see my dead relatives."

Then the servant said, "Are you sure you want to do that, sir?"

The pharaoh replied, "Yes, it'll be fine."

So he went running off to the pyramid and opened the first coffin he saw. There was nothing inside! He looked around, then realised the mummy was behind him...

Rupert Tollet (10)
The Hill Primary School, Caversham

Pyramid Of No Return

Pacing through the humid heat of Egypt, the explorer took a last look at his map before wiping a bead of sweat from his face. The map led him to a secret passage embedded in a vast pyramid. He reluctantly entered the peculiar passage. After crawling through the entrance, there stood before him a room of riches! Suddenly, he heard the sound of movement! Cold sweat trickled down his spine. To his relief, it was a mouse. However, suddenly, out of the depths of mystery, a clammy hand grabbed his shoulder! Throughout the pyramid, there was silence, eerie silence...

Ali Hussaini (10)
The Hill Primary School, Caversham

The Viking Battle

It was a bloodthirsty day and the Vikings were about to have their biggest battle yet! Strong, vicious Norway vs gruesome Denmark. All of a sudden, *clash!* The battle began. The wind was howling and the fighters bashed their swords. For Sigard, this was his first fight. Although very strong, he was still only a boy and after a while, his strength weakened. As he turned to flee, he ran into the biggest, fiercest fighter he'd ever seen! The fighter swung his sword back, only for a ferocious gust of wind to blow him over. Sigard escaped!

Alice Clifford (9)
The Hill Primary School, Caversham

The First Cat To Be Worshipped

In the heat of the midday sun, sand flies were buzzing around like helicopters. Imi the cat was nibbling the pharaoh's foot. The pharaoh was annoyed. Because killing cats was illegal in ancient Egypt, he captured Imi in a bag and crawled into a hole in an unfinished pyramid, thinking she would get buried under the rubble. Unfortunately, Imi had nine lives and he only had one, so he got squashed by a falling rock! When Imi came out, she was wearing the pharaoh's crown. She was taken to the palace and worshipped for the rest of her days!

Imogen Herbert (10)
The Hill Primary School, Caversham

The Darkest Night

I was woken by an ear-splitting noise. An air raid siren! With eyes still half stuck together with sleep, I stumbled down the stairs and darted for the nearest air raid shelter. It was pitch-black and the only thing I could see was flickers of fire in the distance from bombs being dropped over London. The air was thick with the smell of burning buildings. I huddled, scared stiff, next to my mother on the cold, hard, wooden bench. I only stopped worrying when the all-clear siren sounded but as I stepped out, I saw my house was destroyed...

Juniper King (10)
The Hill Primary School, Caversham

Roses

The wind whistled through the branches as the brave men came marching through the forest. Inside each and every soldier was the same thing - fear, fear of what was to come on the battlefield. As they emerged out of the forest, they could see King Richard III and his soldiers in the distance. The king's army was bigger but Henry's army had better soldiers and soon King Richard was lying on the floor. He knew his time had come as he finally fell into a deep sleep.

"All hail King Henry VII, the new King of England!"

Caterina Demiris (10)
The Hill Primary School, Caversham

The Creature Is Coming!

The wind blew strongly as I edged closer and closer towards the temple. My hands itched with trepidation. What was inside? I tiptoed tantalisingly slowly with echoes coming from my footsteps. I heard a groan. I was terrified! Who was it? My heart skipped a beat as I thought it could be a mummy! I froze but did one thing, I looked down and that was when I saw it, a mummy! I thought what to do. It was creeping closer and closer towards me. *Run...*
"Wake up, Tim, it's time to go to school!"
It was a dream!

Ben Attwood-Brown (10)
The Hill Primary School, Caversham

The Titanic

As the sea boomed over the 'unsinkable' boat, many were thrown overboard. Sprinting for my life, I ran for shelter. The air was damp and misty. I was soaked with freezing cold water. I thought I was going to freeze to death! I slipped on the water and skidded on my back. I screamed as I hit a wall. I got up, hearing shouts and commands that were half blocked out by the roaring waves. *Boom!* The whole boat jolted. A shiver went down my spine as the boat started to turn vertical and water flooded in. The Titanic sank...

Riley Chandler (10)
The Hill Primary School, Caversham

Where The Monsters Lurk

A volcano rumbled in the distance and rain poured down. I was running through the jungle. Trees were falling down all around me and mist was curling through the air. The monster was approaching! I looked behind me and razor-sharp teeth, giant claws and bloodthirsty red eyes glared back! I tripped over and rain hit me like a whip. The creature was closing in. I kept on running, nearly being blinded by lightning and deafened by thunder. That was when I saw exactly what the monster was. My blood ran cold. The spinosaurus was there...

Saadiq Alikhan (10)
The Hill Primary School, Caversham

A Fearsome, Frightening Fiend

The strong wind howled around me. I was surrounded by a thick curtain of fog. Suddenly, I heard footsteps. They were too loud to be a human. Then for a second, there was an eerie silence. Suddenly, out of nowhere, there was an ear-splitting, diabolical roar. It was thunderous! I opened my mouth to scream but no sound came out. I could feel tears of fright falling down my face. My heart was beating so fast that I could hear it over the noise. The footsteps were getting closer. I turned around and I saw what it was. A dinosaur...

Zara Jamal (10)
The Hill Primary School, Caversham

WWI

The wind howled and bullets rained down on the muddy trenches of France. Marco was mourning the death of his brother, Manuel. It happened the night before. He said he was doing a check but didn't come back. Later, Marco got told the bad news. Now, he had no one as his parents had also been killed. He had to venture by himself through the war. The rain battered down on Marco and his fellow troops as if it was punishing them. As they walked, they tried to keep their spirits up, yet they didn't know what was to come...

Ayman Adam (10)
The Hill Primary School, Caversham

The Great Tsar Bell

It was the Great Egg Competition in the summer of 1785. The competition was to throw eggs over the Tsar Bell. The eggs that didn't make it got stuck on the scorching bell and fried.

After the competition, there were white splodges from the eggs. One brave soul peeled one off and ate it. He loved it! He called the Tsar to try one. He loved it too! He sent for the city inventor to make a machine to remove the eggs. The machine distributed the eggs to everyone along with a shot of vodka. After all, he was Russian!

Fynn Sebastian Sturk (10)
The Hill Primary School, Caversham

The Lost Poem

A deafening sound screeched in my ears. The air raid siren was sounding. Everyone was screaming. My heart was beating like thunder. I was running for a small, damp air raid shelter. My legs nearly collapsed beneath me.

Finally, I was inside. It was hot and stuffy but I was safe.

As I lay down, I felt a piece of paper scrunched into a ball. I unfolded it and on it was a poem: 'A terrifying war stands under my feet, a poppy I'm clasping to my heart and a new world is in front of me'...

Ruby Riddington (10)
The Hill Primary School, Caversham

The Flood

My family lived hidden from the world. We would always go out on our boat and fish. One day, the water began to rise and we were in trouble! We were saved as we came across an ark built by Noah who was aboard with his family. He told us that God had created the flood to rid the world of evil. We lived on the ark and had many pets until one day, we saw a rainbow which was God's sign the flood was over! Noah's family and my family found land and lived together and became great friends.

Luca Elliot Bundy (10)
The Hill Primary School, Caversham

Where Am I?

There I stood in the extraordinary place of Egypt with my family, but before I knew it, the wind came and I managed to get some brightly-coloured sand in my eyes! My eyes blacked out and all of a sudden, I trembled into a massive house. *No, wait...* My eyes opened. It was a pyramid! Then my brain finally woke up and told me I needed to find my family. All of a sudden, a shadow appeared. "Mum! It's me! Mum?"
Suddenly, I realised it was not Mum...

Sydney Layla Grant (10)
The Hill Primary School, Caversham

Don't Go To The Woods Alone

The rain sprinkled the whole woods clean as the girl strolled through the woods. *Crackle!* she heard. Her nerves took control. She screamed and panicked. Suddenly, the bush was crackling again. She noticed a tiny white paw. Eventually, she noticed it was just a rabbit! All of a sudden, she heard an ear-deafening roar. She sprinted whilst screaming. She tilted her head slightly to her right. She saw a vile, blood-dripping creature. A T-rex! She knew it was all over...

Josh Glister (10)
The Hill Primary School, Caversham

In The Woods

One day, there was a dragon in some woods and it was sleeping on the floor. A while later, two children were walking in the woods. The dragon woke up and saw the children and the dragon tried to hurt them and kill them. One of the children had a sword to kill the dragon. The child who had the sword stabbed the dragon in its side and then blood was coming out of the dragon's body! Then it was on the floor, dead.
"We've killed the dragon!"

Charlie Harvey (9)
The Hill Primary School, Caversham

Terrible Tudors

The wind howled, the trees surged, the rain poured down on me as the glistening, bloodstained axe was about to come down on my neck. I tried blotting out the crowd's jeering and laughing. How could I escape? There looked like there was no way out... Just then, the evil king rose to his feet and everyone turned and stared as he bellowed, "Off with her head!"
I only had a few seconds left if I was to escape. But how?

Chloe Gritten (9)
The Hill Primary School, Caversham

The Last Christian

"Ouch!" someone screamed in agony.

As I looked over at where the scream was coming from, all I saw were giant candles, some bigger than others. Next to one of the shorter ones, I spotted Nero howling with laughter.

"What are these?" I asked, looking at the unusual candles.

"They're Christians! Don't they look beautiful?" he replied.

He was right, they were Christians.

Looking closer, I saw one was wearing a cross on his neck.

"You're not Christian are you?"

"No!" I said in fear.

As fast as a racing tiger, I ran... straight into one of Nero's royal guards...

Cameron Maskell (11)
Trevelyan Middle School, Windsor

Ugg

"Today, Ugg will teach you to kill mammoth. Step one: throw spear. Step two: attack mammoth. Step three: rip it. Ugg throw, Ugg attack, Ugg throw spear... Ugg run, Ugg attack again," Ugg said. "Ugg make up more steps. Step four: get friends. Step five: all throw spear. Step six: all attack. Step seven: run!" Ugg failed again. "Ugg's step eight: try again." Ugg tried to kill the mammoth 1,111 times. "Step nine: give up." Ugg gave up.

"Ugg look out, behind you!" Ugg was crushed. Ugg was dead! "Well, Ugg is dead. He lived a sad, sad life."

Ehsan Chandhar (10)
Trevelyan Middle School, Windsor

Running Far

The wind echoed in my ear, stones tumbled down the hill and trees shook. Suddenly, I froze with fear. Out of the corner of my eye, I saw something white. I was terrified that this something would eat me! I ran for my life but the monster chased after me. I thought, *I'm going to get eaten!* I closed my eyes with fear.

"Argh!" screamed the beast.

I noticed that the beast was covered in what looked like toilet paper that was ripped everywhere. It had bulging blue eyes. I screamed as loud as I could. It was a mummy...

Katie Fry (10)
Trevelyan Middle School, Windsor

Silence At Christmas

The silence echoed throughout the smoky air. The war had stopped! We took a glance outside. There was no fighting, no bombs, no destruction. Soldiers were emerging from their trenches, huddling together and grouping to talk. It was Christmas. The war had stopped for Christmas and it felt brilliant! It was as if there hadn't been silence for an eternity. All you could hear were the subtle whispers of the excited soldiers and the howling of the wind.

"Could it be a surprise attack?" people were whispering, but it wasn't.

It had finally stopped... just for a day.

Isaac Jansen (11)
Trevelyan Middle School, Windsor

The Wrapped Person

"Oh yes, we have finished. See you tomorrow. I'm going home now," muttered Kathrin.

"Okay," muttered Jack.

Jack was just about to get into his car when he spotted a figure wrapped in what looked like old masking tape. It had terrifying eyes bulging out.

"I will eat you!" the figure bellowed at Jack.

Frightened, Jack screamed like a girl and jumped out of his car. Luckily, Kathrin spotted the monster and tossed him to the ground. The mummy got angrier and angrier and almost ate Kathrin alive! How were they ever going to get out alive?

Sydnie Maclaughlin (10)
Trevelyan Middle School, Windsor

Mummy Mayhem

As Tilly reached into the ancient tomb, she tugged out a block of gold. She looked up and saw the walls slowly disintegrating! Suddenly, she heard a noise.

"Come out!" she shouted as her voice echoed through the pyramid.

Within a second, Tilly felt a hand on her.

"Argh!" she screamed.

Trembling with fear, she found herself face-to-face with a blood-dripping figure with very sharp teeth that could kill her in seconds! As she sprinted, all she could see was white linen brushing her in the face. Then she came to a dead end and got dragged under...

Kitty Warren (10)
Trevelyan Middle School, Windsor

Virtual Horror

Our eyes were agog as we stared at the screen and clutched fluffy pillows to our chests. The Viking's axe gleamed with blood in the moonlight. She bared her teeth at the camera. They looked yellower than cheese. She was coming towards us and she wasn't stopping! The screams deafened me as the tip of her axe cut through the screen and into my friend's room! Sprinting downstairs, we desperately looked for a hiding place. I counted the screams echoing around the house. Opening the door, the last thing I could see was the wicked grin across her face...

Delphi Perkins (11)
Trevelyan Middle School, Windsor

Mummy Chase

Whoosh, whoosh! The storm of sand was getting closer and closer. I was running from the creature. It had black holes for eyes and it was creating the storm! Blood was dripping from its ragged clothes. Balls of sand were now bombing down on me, making explosions. In front, there was an upright pyramid. Running towards it, my feet sunk into the ground. The creature was now running like a maniac. It looked like it was going to collapse. Turning around towards the pyramid, I saw there were 100 more of these death-defying creatures. They were mummies...

Oliver Comley (10)
Trevelyan Middle School, Windsor

Run!

The hairs on our necks stood up. The banging intensity increased. Out of the corner of my eye, I saw white linen start to cover my vision. Our jaws dropped, our bodies froze. The beasts stood there with bloody jaws, maintaining eye contact. Soon after, 1,000 more burst through the door, moaning. As quick as a flash, we were face-to-face with the monsters. They were all dressed in the same white linen and all that was noticeable were pairs of ruby-red eyes. *Bang!* My friends all dropped to the floor. It was a herd of mummies...

Lybah Hussain (10)
Trevelyan Middle School, Windsor

The Beasts Within The Tomb

Cautiously, I crept towards the brooch (a golden brooch in the shape of a crucifix with a red gem on) with my dog, Greg, trotting behind me. Suddenly, a giant axe swung out of nowhere and barely missed me! I stumbled and grabbed the brooch.

Immediately, the coffins in the tomb burst open and monsters with green mutated eyes, wrapped in silk, came charging towards me! As quick as a flash, Greg ran back to the exit. Suddenly, Greg fell over and I ran back to help but the monsters gained on us. I screamed. The monsters were mummies...

Willem Max Murphy (10)

Trevelyan Middle School, Windsor

WWII Escape

I was dragged, dragged away into the half-blown up building with rats as guests by the cruel killer Germans who'd stop at nothing in making the Englishmen's lives a misery. Soon, I was chucked into the jail. My face was as sore as fire. It was very cold as all I was wearing was my thin jacket.
I was to escape that night!
Later, I picked the lock of my cell, ran down the stairs, down to the snowy earth. However, I was being chased by the rumbling steel machine that would stop at nothing in its path - a tank...

Tom Crossland (10)
Trevelyan Middle School, Windsor

The Tomb Of Doom

In a dark time, long ago, an explorer was looking for the treasure of the mummy. Shivering in fear, he entered the tomb and started to step forwards. In the corner, he could see the shimmer of gold! All of a sudden, a mummy came out of nowhere! He ran and ran until there was a dead end.

"Help!" he shouted but no one could hear him. Then the mummy grabbed him by the feet and pulled him into his lair. Each day that followed, more and more people went missing searching for the treasure...

Grace Anne Clarke (11)
Trevelyan Middle School, Windsor

The Second World War Commences

As I strolled into the camp, my hands began to feel numb. I was feeling lonely. A generous person saw my hands and gave me some hot chocolate. He started talking to me about how his father had died in WWI and that he wanted to fight for him now. All of a sudden, I heard the screeching of bombs falling and we rushed for safety. Just a fraction away from us, a bomb landed from the sky and sent pieces of shrapnel flying that went in every direction.

As I awoke, I saw my new friend lying helplessly...

Ibrahim Niaz (11)
Trevelyan Middle School, Windsor

The Stone Age Tale

There I was, standing in what seemed like the Stone Age. I walked and walked and walked and then I heard footsteps as loud as a lion's roar. "Argh!" I screamed.

It was a caveman! He said his name was Ugg and he said he was lonely so I said he could be my friend. After that, I continued with my journey to get home. Then I saw something. It had blood around its face and razor-sharp teeth staring me in the eye! I couldn't move, I was stuck. It was a sabre-toothed tiger...

Poppy Warren (10)

Trevelyan Middle School, Windsor

I Awoke

The darkness surrounded me as I awoke from the dead. As my eyes lit, I felt trepidation climb up me. I tried to bust the lock. I finally accomplished my mission. My bones cracked like when you snap pencils. I got up and looked around. I thought I was in Cairo. I heard people outside. Around me, I saw treasure: cat statues, jewels and gold. There was a huge cat on top of my tomb It was gold, black and shiny. The pyramid I was in was made from gold and it shone in the light. I was a mummy!

Marissa Gaynor (11)
Trevelyan Middle School, Windsor

Fifty Years Since I Went To The Moon

I saw my first glimpse of our destination. I could see a shimmer of light. My heart skipped a breath with pride as I carried on, my helmet in my arms. A shimmering figure was standing before me. We took off as if it was a volcano erupting. It was the most thunderous ride of my life! The moon reflected in my eyes. As my jaw dropped, I saw a million craters everywhere. When I planted the flag, I could see my great-grandchild in my vision as if he was standing there next to me!

Bronwen Crick (11)
Trevelyan Middle School, Windsor

The Thief

It was a dark, windy day on the streets of England. Amelia was trying to steal fruits from the market but the thing was that the castle for King Henry VIII was right in front of the market! There were lots of people in the castle who saw Amelia trying to steal food. They tried to catch Amelia in the market. Amelia didn't hesitate and just ran! Amelia was way too fast for the guards but then she ran into a dead end. Amelia knew what was going to happen next... Execution!

Omory Samms (9)
Trevelyan Middle School, Windsor

The Killer Bomb

I was dragged, dragged by the killer Germans. I felt near death. They dragged me like a scaly chameleon. I could hear a bang going off. The Germans put me in a POW camp. There was a gigantic number of people in there. I was scared, very scared. I didn't know what to do. I decided to get out. All of a sudden, I heard that bang going off again. I ran as fast as I could to get out of the mess I was in. The noise was deafening. It was a bomb, heading right towards me...

Freddie Burchell (10)
Trevelyan Middle School, Windsor

Dogfight

As I jumped into the plane and took off, I heard the sound of machine guns piercing wood as planes were being shot. Suddenly, my plane began to cough and splutter and I struggled to control it. Narrowly, I missed the enemy's fire. Would I be that lucky again? Shots hit the side of the plane. I was in a dogfight! Suddenly, the plane began to descend at the speed of light. All around me were planes that were descending with canvas trailing behind them...

Charlie Burlison (11)
Trevelyan Middle School, Windsor

Witchcraft!

It was a wet and windy day as Farmer Bob raced inside his hut. Bob started to make his dinner when he heard a crash. Bob hurried to his bedroom to check it. It was all messed up and a cat was sitting on his bed... a black cat!
"Call the Witchfinder General!"
Bob rushed back to the kitchen and all his food had gone mouldy and his milk had gone lumpy. Out of the corner of his eye, he could see a pointy hat in the corner of the room...

Cassius Wise (10)
Trevelyan Middle School, Windsor

The Crazy Mummy

Long ago in ancient Egypt, something weird happened. It was a normal day and, as usual, Egypt shimmered in the sun. People were buying food with the little money they had.
Suddenly, they heard someone scream, "Mummy!" It was so loud that some people's ears were bleeding! To their surprise, there was a walking mummy wrapping people up and putting them in coffins!
He was screaming, "Ha ha, payback!"
He carried on one by one until there was only one girl left. She ran and climbed up the nearest tree and stayed safe.

Jaylin Boubker (9)
Western House Academy, Cippenham

The Mummies Are Back!

One cold, shadowy night, Lily was working late. *Bang, bang!* She heard a knock on her door.
"Let us in!"
Trying not to scream, she looked through the peephole and said, "Hello?" in the most scared voice ever. She then realised the mummies were back!
"Oh no!" she screamed whilst her heart skipped a beat.
She looked through the window. They were ruining everything outside! The mummy invasion had started again! By the time Lily had looked away, the mummies had managed to break the door down and come in. She was frightened. As quick as lightning, she hid...

Aaisha Giri (8)
Western House Academy, Cippenham

The Pharaoh

He woke up. His slaves were surrounding him. The pharaoh demanded food. The second he looked around, *bang!* The room vibrated rapidly. Slaves dropped onto the floor. The pharaoh's coffin fell. He looked outside. The building that took one year to build, collapsed. The pharaoh ran. Then, he couldn't believe his eyes. A dragon with dark red eyes flew around Egypt. Slaves fell off buildings. He couldn't be stopped. He flew to the pharaoh's palace. One breath he took, fire came out. As soon as the hot substance touched the pharaoh, he was only seen in the afterlife.

Dawand Sirwan Jamal Rashid (10)
Willow Tree Primary School, Northolt

The Day Dinosaurs Once Walked

The year 3020 began and my immensely stubborn brother really wanted to make a time machine. He's stupid. The next thing I knew, I was pushed in. *Thump!* Groaning loudly, I stared around and I saw I was in the Jurassic period. *Stomp!*
Stomp! Turning around, I glimpsed a T-rex. I screamed louder than I'd ever screamed and ran...
Splash! I thought they wouldn't be able to swim the murky depths of the sea, so I used my strength to swim away into a peculiar cave... full of stalagmites. Oh no! I'd swum into the ravenous jaws of an ichthystega!

Anjali Kumar (11)
Willow Tree Primary School, Northolt

Tomb

Back in 2000BC, Moses and Ramsey III were best friends. One day, they had been bored, so they decided to steal jewels from an ancient pharaoh's tomb.

Two days later, they had found their disguise. Today was the day that they got the jewels. Slowly, they opened the tomb. The pungent smell had invaded their nose and tongue. They had searched and searched, but still, nothing. Slowly, they opened the tomb and a mummy jumped out! "Argh!" they screamed.

Bang! Crack! There was blood everywhere and their heads were gone!

Ali Shidane (11)
Willow Tree Primary School, Northolt

Today Is The Day

That was it, locked up forever. What was I thinking? Maybe stealing wasn't a good idea, even when you're in ancient Egypt. I'm stuck here now.
One week later...
"Come on, wake up, today is the day!" said a voice.
"Today is the day for what?" I asked.
"It is beheading day!" said the voice who was the executioner.
Downstairs, ready to die, I said, "Tell my mum I love her!"
Chop! Chop! Chop! My mum wasn't told I was dead. She couldn't come to the funeral.

Iman Yassaa (10)
Willow Tree Primary School, Northolt

The Grand Entrance

Yikes! New year, less food. We were all struggling in 1700BC. Lots of mammoths dying, why couldn't they stop? Me and my so-called Pa had been boiling insects! It was absolutely bonkers, eating rabbit poo didn't taste as good as mammoth! My pa was out of the cave one day in his 'wheel' (people were literally dying to ride his wheel, maybe it was because lots of diseases were out there)! Sadly, my pa died because he came across shiny people wearing a fascinating material. That is when the Stone Age ended and the Bronze Age began!

Nelly Siddiqi (10)
Willow Tree Primary School, Northolt

Ancient Giant Tree Spider Of All

Back in ancient times, when unknown creatures were found in different countries, when it was millions and millions of years ago in China, people found a forest that was moving impossibly. They thought dinosaurs were still alive, but dinosaurs only had two to four legs and this had eight. Everyone thought it was evil because it leaked tree poison. People thought no one would survive but, as they all looked at it, it was friendly. It was a giant creature. They saw it had four teeth and this mystery creature was a giant tree spider.

Nojus Arminas (10)
Willow Tree Primary School, Northolt

The Day I Lost My Head

It was a wonderful day. I had just had a baby girl. It was the happiest time of my life. All until my lovely husband, King Henry VIII, came in. He was furious! He ordered his guards to take me to prison. I heard him screaming about a boy. I was too shocked to stop the guards dragging me down the steep stairs. After a painful three days in the worst place, prison, I was finally taken out to see my worst nightmare. The crowd cheered. They put me on my knees. I felt a sharp pain... a cheer, darkness...

Robert Bunker (10)
Willow Tree Primary School, Northolt

The Ancient Mummy

It all started when a small girl called Lina woke up in the middle of a desert. Lost. Alone. There was no one there to help her. Lina's mother was lost and she really wanted to find her, so Lina stood up, feeling confident. After a while, she saw a pyramid in the distance, a huge, massive one. Lina began to run towards it as fast as she could. Once she got there, she slowly opened the door. Lina saw a mummy. She ran. Then, she realised it was someone familiar. It was her mother. She was so so happy!

Maryam Baloch (10)
Willow Tree Primary School, Northolt

The Minotaur

It was a day like no other. The sun stretched through the dry land. It had been a week since I'd been searching for the horrendous minotaur that was lurking around this area last month. I couldn't walk another mile as I felt really weak. That's when I saw it. The old, dusty grave of the minotaur. My mouth dropped. I quickly sprinted towards the grave. Suddenly, the minotaur's arm came out of the grave and its sharp claws slashed me on my face. Since then, I haven't been found...

Faizan Arshad (10)
Willow Tree Primary School, Northolt

Dino The Dinosaur

It all started with me running for my life from Dino the dinosaur. He slowly started running faster and started opening his mouth. As soon as I thought things couldn't get any worse, they did. The Bee's Knees team came out - they were not nice, I can tell you that! I somehow got past them, but Dino the dinosaur was getting closer by the minute. Then, out of nowhere, gorilla men came out and told me to get on their backs. After I got on, we ran into the sun.

Stephen Pavel Thomas (10)
Willow Tree Primary School, Northolt

The Rampage

I was sleeping in my bed until I heard a rampage. It became louder and louder. Suddenly, *thump!* My books came tumbling down and there, I saw it, a T-rex looking straight at me. I was trying to scream but no sound came out. I tried again, only a little bit of a scream came out. No one could hear it because everyone had been eaten beside me. No wonder there were only earthquakes these days and no other sounds. I already felt like I'd been devoured.

Adiyta Kumar (8)
Willow Tree Primary School, Northolt

The Dragon And The Girl

One day, a girl named Sara was sleeping in her room but she woke up in the desert! She heard stuff, she didn't know what it was. She started walking around and saw a shadow. Sara scurried. Following it, she chased it. It was a dragon! It started to not be nice to the girl. The girl liked the dragon but the dragon did not know how to talk so the girl started to teach the dragon. The dragon started to like the girl so the girl and the dragon were friends!

Clara Craciun (8)
Willow Tree Primary School, Northolt

Deadly Chase

I was running as fast as my legs could carry me. I wondered every now and then why I got chased by a mysterious Viking who wanted me beheaded because I'm God's son. The wind howled. It was night. Stiff rocks and fallen trees were in my way. Thick fog shrouded the forest and made it harder for me to see. After a long time of running, I saw a log that I couldn't get over. I had to turn left. I looked and it was a trap...

Jeshan Jegatheeswaran (9)
Willow Tree Primary School, Northolt

The Dinosaur Argument About The Meatball

Once upon a time, there lived a great king T-rex. He didn't let the allosaurus or the raptors eat the giant meatball which was bigger than the Titanic. Then he changed his mind so he shared the meatball with them and they were friends and they decided to share stuff together so they didn't starve. They were good friends and they mostly spent time with each other and hunted different animals.

Dominik Sebastian Adamczyk (9)
Willow Tree Primary School, Northolt

YOUNG WRITERS
INFORMATION

We hope you have enjoyed reading this book – and
that you will continue to in the coming years.

If you're a young writer who enjoys reading and
creative writing, or the parent of an enthusiastic poet
or story writer, do visit our website
www.youngwriters.co.uk. Here you will find free
competitions, workshops and games, as well as
recommended reads, a poetry glossary and our blog.

If you would like to order further copies of
this book, or any of our other titles give us a
call or visit **www.youngwriters.co.uk**.

Young Writers
Remus House
Coltsfoot Drive
Peterborough
PE2 9BF

(01733) 890066
info@youngwriters.co.uk

 YoungWritersUK

 @YoungWritersCW